Kin

*A day in the lives of
a father and son – and
everything else in-between*

ACORN BOOKS

Scott Tierney

First published in 2019 by
Acorn Books
www.acornbooks.co.uk

Acorn Books is an imprint of
Andrews UK Limited
www.andrewsuk.com

Contents

Kin

One

For a second time, the father whispered his final culminating words into the ear of his beloved wife.

He absorbed her. Captured her for posterity.

She looked up to the ceiling – the pillow supporting her head was rough, inexpensive, and smelt of disinfectant.

All the same, she stroked the gold signet ring on the old man's little finger…

He clasped her hands and tenderly kissed each individual knuckle, taking care not to dislodge the cannula bandaged tightly around her wrist.

All crows feet and lolly stick teeth, he produced one of his winning smiles.

His better smiles.

Leaning across the bed, he asked that she hurry back.

"We'll still be here." he assured, adjusting the lay of her hair across the pillow – soft and delicate, as dear as gold.

"Right outside, waiting for you.

"Then, when you're ready, we'll take the car home.

"All three of us."

The wife smiled – but didn't reply.

Nothing further was said…

The surrounding curtains parted.

There came a tap on the father's elbow.

He didn't turn around.

Not just yet.

Nonetheless, the porters moved in and took hold of the bed…

The father stepped aside. Made way. He blew his wife a kiss over the porter's shoulders.

She didn't see it.

In one practised manoeuvre the bed was rotated from the ward and rolled down the adjoining corridor, the wheels quivering and squeaking like abandoned hatchlings.

Surgeons in battle dress arrived alongside the bed, comparing notes and procedures and jokes. Nurses soon joined at the flanks.

The father followed a few paces behind, watching his wife intently – he noticed that each time she passed under the glare of a ceiling light, she winced…

A nurse beside the bed prescribed comment on the typical weather, a proverbial comfort blanket.

Yet the wife kept her eyes closed. Bit her lip.

Her bare hands fidgeted on her belly.

They'd asked her to remove all her jewellery beforehand…

The train gathered momentum – schedule rather than emergency. Onwards past windows streaked with the summer morning's unseasonal rain.

Empty beds lined the walls of the corridor. On the corner of one bed a middle-aged man was perched, loitering, toying with his phone.

Noticing the train pass, he stood and caught up to it.

Hurriedly, he said something to the wife.

She smiled. Replied. Before the man was asked to step aside, she kissed his chin.

The father didn't catch what either said…

At the end of the corridor awaited a set of blue double-doors, each with a frosted window and a strip of dented metal across the bottom third.

With a bang, the head of the bed was driven between them, forcing the doors apart.

The wife flinched.

The doors swung closed.

The father could go no further.

He was faintly breathless.

"Did your mother seem in good spirits to you?" he asked the middle aged man across the corridor.

"Comfortable. Considering." he replied in a Mancunian drawl, joining his father at his side.

He wiped the lipstick from his chin.

"Content, I'd guess."

The father glanced to his son, the red stain.

"And what reason would she have not to be."

As it wasn't deemed a question, the son didn't provide an answer…

With a final scroll, he slipped his phone into the pocket of his leather jacket, then coughed.

Behind the doors, blinds were drawn across glass.

A genuine question from the father:

"Did you give the nurses your number, so they can contact us the moment anything happens?"

The son was still coughing.

"The right number?" the father added.

"Yeah."

"None of the usual cock-up?"

"No."

"You're sure?"

"For fuc—"

The son held his tongue.

They were in public…

"I gave them the number, Pops. They'll reach out if they have to."

The father exhaled through his nose. He was still looking at the blue doors.

That glass.

Those blinds…

Against the corridor wall was a bench – little more than four sheets of cheap green plastic with holes in the legs. The father sat himself down, leant back, hands clasped between knees.

Set between framed watercolour paintings, a clock ticked on the opposite wall. The old man compared his watch to it.

Quarter to nine. Correct.

Rain pit-a-patted at the windows like fingernails on a headmaster's desk.

The son yawned…

"I'm going for a puff." he muttered, pulling a damp box of cigarettes from his pocket and thrusting a long one between his lips.

As he spoke, the cigarette wagged.

"You'll still be here?"

Adjusting his glasses, the father looked up to the information board on the wall.

"There's a cafeteria along the way." he observed, ensuring the son had taken note.

"Alright. Meet you there."

"Perhaps I'll join you." the father suggested, moving to rise.

Yet the son was already half way down the corridor...

The father sat back down. He folded his arms and looked off into the distance.

Long before he was outside, the son had already lit his first cigarette of the day.

Two

It was the height of summer – yet the rain fell in buckets.
Rivers. Lakes.

The dumping of a fucking ocean…

As cold a rain as only a Northern rain. That frigid, scentless, inescapable torrent which plummets in streaks. Which pelts every surface like bottles hurled against stage – the sound reminiscent of far gone applause.

In this weather, no one ventured out without good reason.

Not unless it was absolutely necessary.

Hospitals were the exception.

As was family…

Leaning under the hospital entrance's brick canopy, the son watched an ambulance pull up outside A&E, tyres skidding.

The rear doors burst open – a child on a stretcher was spat out, followed by its mother.

As the paramedics wheeled the patient inside, the mother took off her coat and used it to shield her child from the rain.

By the time she'd reached the doors, she was soaked through.

The son could see her breasts through her blouse…

He drew on his cigarette.

Shivered.

Stamped his feet.

This morning's visitor's to the hospital looked regrettable – scuttling from cars, checking their watches, shaking dry their umbrellas as they ducked into the foyer.

More went in than came out, the son noted:

One half of an elderly couple.

A wife minus a husband.

A newborn in the arms of a single parent…

The son's eyes glazed over…

A lodging cough awoke him like a slap – such was the surprise, he almost fumbled his fag.

He finished what remained and trod it into the ground, twisting it to paste.

Checking the time on his phone, he considered going back inside and joining his father.

He'd be waiting.

"He hates to be kept waiting…"

But it had only been a few minutes.

Barely five.

If that…

Fuck it – the son lit another cigarette.

No harm. He had the whole day.

Besides, no one else under the canopy seemed compelled to return…

The smokers – a mass of raincoats huddled together like grey penguins. Patients and relatives and taxi drivers and staff – on breaks and taking breaks from the harsh realities of life.

They coughed together. Wheezed together. Shared one-another's fumes.

Yet no one conversed – not a word.

Everyone understood the unspoken rule, the silent law:

Privacy.

No one had come out here to make friends or congress or chew over the turmoil of their day-to-day existence with like-minded strangers.

They came only to smoke.

To escape.

For five precious minutes.

And then, one by one, they would gradually return to what awaited them…

But not just yet.

One more cigarette would make no difference.

"One for luck." the son muttered to himself, his breath a mixture of condensation and smoke.

"One for the road…"

The son leant closer to the wall – James Dean of the North, Matalan Morrissey.

He shivered. Coughed. He wrapped the collar of his leather jacket tight around his throat, pinning it in place with his chin.

Between puffs he blew on his hands as though the chill could be dispelled like dust.

Balls deep into his forties and still he hadn't learnt to dress suitably...

Dress fashionably? He liked to think so. And he liked to think that others thought so, too.

He scrubbed up well.

For his age.

For the mileage.

But not for this rain...

It got everywhere: under his bracelets and in-between the laces of his neon trainers and across the print of his distressed t-shirt and into every crevice exemplified by his skinny jeans, causing the denim to stick to his crotch like cling film over leftover drumsticks.

At least the jacket was waterproof – the rain skipped clean off the leather. But the leather, despite the price, was thin, worn, no more insulating than the skin of an avocado.

Not even his excess weight, his Majorca-paunch, kept him cosy...

He wiped his glasses on the hem of his t-shirt, then reapplied them over sunken eyes – now they were smudged... milky blemishes across dark, tinted lenses.

An icy bead trickled down the centre of his large sloping nose.

It was bent out of place. Broken like a mast.

The result of an altercation when he was a boy...

"This rain," he cursed between chattering teeth.

"Will it ever end?"

By his third cigarette, it hadn't...

With simmering frustration the son trod another filter into the ground, and re-checked the time on his phone.

As though disturbed, it rang.

The thumbnail of a sultry young girl reclining across a public wash basin appeared on screen.

The photo had been taken under blue light. Late night.

After a few too many...

The phone continued to ring.

Before answering, the son's thumb dithered between a left and right swipe...

"How's it going, babe?" he began with eagerness, raising his voice over the traffic and rain – but not enough to disturb the smokers.

"Really?

"You don't say.

"Half the night, huh…"

Woe is she…

"Same old. She's just gone in.

"Nothing major. Routine. In and out in a day.

"But you know how Pops gets.

"No. It can't be easy for him.

"Can't be…"

He fiddled with the ring on his left hand.

The rain had worked it loose.

"No, I didn't get a chance.

"And she wouldn't have wanted me to.

"No.

"No…

"…that's all in the past…"

No use in arguing…

A quick spark and reload.

While she vents, he intakes…

"What's the plan for tonight, anyway? Me, you and the telly? That Netflix if you like.

"Hungry? Peckish?

"Thirsty! Now you're talking!

"Don't know what time I'll be able to get away, so…

"Run dry? I thought we had a few stashed around the back of—

"Oh yeah. Friday.

"Touch of the wet-brain.

"As always…

"In that case I'll pick-up a couple of bottles on the way back. Unless you've got time?"

Excuses. Strapped. Lean pockets on leaner hips.

"No, I'll make it stretch – I put a couple of extra shifts in last week. And the summer coppers are nearly upon us.

"Jingling like ice in fucking Sangría…

"Oh, and there's been another gig." the son added with keenness. "Did I mention how well it went? The gig?"

8

He had…

"Right, well… I'll call you later if anything changes, then…

"Hopefully I won't have to…"

Silence.

"…you know that's not what I meant.

"Why would it be a hassle?

"Why wouldn't I want—"

He snatched the cigarette from his mouth.

"It cuts both ways, Elly!"

Petulantly, the son swiped the girl's portrait off screen, set the phone to silent, and stuffed it back inside his jacket.

"Fucking bitch…"

He began coughing again.

In an instinctive reflex he reached into his breast pocket – inside, day and night, rain or shine, there was always a remedy:

Gold crest.

Green glass.

Maroon cap.

Amber nectar.

When making contact with his ring, the bottle emitted a hollow chime.

Empty.

Shit…

The son shivered.

One by one, the smokers were trudging back inside.

With heavy legs, the son begrudgingly did the same.

Three

Too early for lunch, too late for breakfast – the hospital cafeteria was spacious and in a prolonged state of inactivity. Noiseless due to its vacancy like an empty guitar case.

The vapour of wholesale coffee permeated every corner, steaming up the windows.

Used tea cups clattered together on a trolley.

Recently doused disinfectant was enough to choke…

Yawning doctors were glossing their paperwork, while visitors leafed last month's supplements. Some sat in couples. Most were alone. Few spoke – and when they did they were mindful to keep their voices lowered, so as not to infringe on the hush.

A television on the furthest wall broadcast daytime TV.

It was muted.

Behind yellow subtitles, a roguish and unshaven detective was hunkered on a stakeout.

It was an old episode. Early 70s. Formerly primetime and hard hitting – now relegated to the position of interstitial.

A handful of people were watching at a distance, glancing up every few minutes.

They weren't missing much…

Tentatively yet with reinforced swank, the son cut a path across the room.

The father was occupying a table by the window.

Back turned to the TV.

Festering.

Waiting…

The son knew a bollocking was on the cards. A tongue lashing. A public dressing down in relation to his tardiness.

Being forty was no protection. No excuse.

Those who behaved like children would be treated as such...

Yet when he reached the table, the son found his father to be in a jovial persuasion – as jubilant as a peacock.

So much can be masked behind feathers of technicolor...

"Eh up, David! So nice of you to finally join us."

Regional slang – a bad sign...

"I'd like to introduce Mr. and Mrs. Stanlow." the father announced in theatrical bravado. "Lovely people. Local people. Born and bred on the cobbles just down the road from here. Both have braved the weather for their annual check-up, so they tell me."

An old couple at the next table smiled cordially, acknowledging the son as one would a neighbour's budgie...

At a glance, the Stanlows resembled one another to an uncanny degree:

They wore identical sheepskin coats toggled around their throats like nooses.

Both had glossy white hair. Large ears.

And squashed, attentive eyes.

From their table they considered the son's face inquisitively. Inspected it. Compared it. They looked to one another, sharing a private conception...

"Say hello, David." the father instructed.

"Hello, David..." the son replied.

He always spoke as though chewing a piece of gum...

Nonetheless, the son exchanged pleasantries with the old couple – while glancing to the TV, albeit.

"Wet one, eh?" he muttered, thumbing the nearby window.

"Bitter weather." stated Mr. Stanlow. "No getting away from it. Not good for the chest."

"Not good at all." added Mrs. Stanlow, cradling her tea between puffy red-varnished fingers. "Like an icy bath. Bad for the blood."

"Bad for the chest."

"Bad for all."

"Is that so?" the son commented as though an exertion, hands in pockets, mind elsewhere.

On the TV, the detective was attempting to infiltrate a black gang by acting street.

He was over-egging the part...

"The Stanlows and I were just discussing," the father mused, leaning back over his chair, "How easily one can lose themselves in these wretched hospitals.

"Weren't we just saying that?"

Grinning, the old couple nodded in agreement.

Bowed, practically.

"Yes, Mr. Atherton."

"Quite so, Mr. Atherton."

The father raised a hand.

"Please. Just David will suffice."

"Of course, Mr. David."

Sponges – adding nothing but absorbing everything, the son belittled of the couple.

Had they jotters they would have taken notes…

"But yes, these hospitals – warren-like structures." the father continued in that RADA trained tongue, his voice for the back rows.

Tellingly muddied with colliery smut…

"A spider's web they so seem.

"Labyrinthine.

"A catacomb.

"A proverbial ants nest of windows and wards from which there is no apparent escape."

The Stanlows nodded eagerly.

"Bitter places." one said.

"Bitter." echoed the other.

"Is that so?.." yawned the son, air wheezing from a balloon.

"And these corridors – ever so poorly lit, I might add." the father continued. "Such is the sobering tenebrosity one struggles to see beyond the tip of their nose.

"I assume that is the reason why you took so long to locate us?" the father accused, turning unexpectedly towards his son, all ruler and readied cane.

"What's that?" the son sniffed.

"You misplaced yourself in this maze, lad.

"Came over all befuddled and anxious.

"Found yourself wanting.

"Or do you propose an ulterior excuse for your retarded punctuality?"

As though a bank holiday drama playing out before them, the Stanlows awaited the son's response…

The two men, the father and son, were unblinking.

Gunfighters. Heavyweights. Stags.

The old couple leant in, pressed their noses to the screen, anticipating fisticuffs, antlers, cordite.

Blood.

Yet the son roundly disappointed them – there would be no altercation this early into the episode.

"Yeah, if you like, Pops." he exhaled, dropping into the seat across from his father.

He unbuttoned his jacket, and ran his fingers through his thinning black-dyed hair.

"Sounds about right. I got lost. Lost like you wouldn't believe."

He'd like to thank the academy…

"Just couldn't keep track of myself."

"He never can." the father remarked smugly to the couple. "Family trait, I'm afraid."

He wiped his palms together as though dirtied with soil.

"From his mother's side."

The Stanlows chuckled.

The father shared in it.

The detective marched into his local, slapped down his badge, and began holding court…

"I remember an occasion in the late sixties when his aforementioned mother and I became separated in Fortnum & Masons."

"Harrods…" the son corrected.

The father continued.

"We'd arrived one evening to collect a picnic basket—"

"Hamper…"

"For Christmas—"

"Easter…"

"And, bless her heart, my beloved wife ended up causing a scene by getting herself imprisoned in the conveniences!"

The son knew this to be bollocks – it was in fact he who had become locked in the toilets, and his mother, who was heavily pregnant at the time, had been left to find help while the father was busy fluttering his plumage for the trainees behind the service desk.

But why let the facts get in the way of a good story?..

The son aimed his attention towards the tittering old couple – he did little to disguise his weariness of their mere presence.

Greedy lap dogs drooling over their master's plates…

"Far from here, your check-up?" he asked as though a demand.

"Not too far out of our way." Mrs. Stanlow answered, cheerfully sipping her tea – a sparrow taking pecks from a bathtub.

"Soon?" the son furthered.

"Soon's we make a move. Once we're fit and ready."

"Well, don't let me keep you…"

Peering at his son over the rim of his mug, the father took a long pull of his tea.

The son was unperturbed…

"Which building?" he pressed all the harder.

"Can't be certain."

"Close by?"

"Would think so."

"And on this floor?

"Same building?

"Distant ward?

"Or will you be scurrying to the other side of the nest with the rest of the rats?"

The father brought down his mug.

"You'll have to excuse this lad of mine." he pardoned, turning his back squarely to his son. "Etiquette has never been his strongest suit."

Cocking a deaf 'un, said lad took a napkin from the stash on the table and wiped his glasses.

"Not entirely his fault, I'll add." the father did so add. "It's being out in public, you see. Brings out the worst in him. Causes him to shrink. Turn to wax. When the occasion arises he's like a mole cowering from the sun."

The detective laughed heartily and downed another double.

"Of course, he's getting better at it – he's endeavouring to interact like a regular member of society.

"Isn't that right, David? Every time we meet you seem a little more open.

"A little more chatty.

"A little less yourself."

The son refused to indulge.

Sticks and stones…

Following a cough, he wiped his mouth on another napkin.

This he scrunched deeply into his pocket…

"Shy, you see." the father deemed proven. "An introvert.

"Just like his mother."

The Stanlows giggled, cocooning their rumps for the feature presentation.

"But as a lad, this little pygmy," the father tutted, sucking his lips. "My word… a bloody firecracker! Short on fuse and big on powder! So many grand occasions disrupted when he went up in smoke!"

Another double downed. Another brutal joke. Another muted cackle.

The son had seen this episode one too many times…

"Would you believe," the father teased, hitting his stride, "In the early seventies I had to chase this scrawny whippersnapper half-naked through Soho on account of him having thrown his dungarees at Diana Rigg. Can you imagine my shame?"

The Stanlows' belly laughs suggested that they could.

"All the way from Palace to Queen's! In broad daylight!"

A well-timed sip prolonged the old couple's hysterics, before the punchline was delivered thus:

"I'm told she still has the dungarees."

Laughing.

Roaring.

The slamming of a jail cell…

The Stanlows swam in each of their host's tales. Paddled in them.

Like pigs in fucking shite…

They needed putting out of their misery, the son reasoned.

So did he…

He reached into his trouser pocket for alleviation.

The cigarette box was wet and empty.

Brilliant…

And half an hour later, the father was still waffling.

Regurgitating story after story.

Titbit after titbit.

Around and around like a scratched 45.

The old man always acted like this when blessed with an audience.

A gathering.

When he'd had a few…

In a weary reverence the son watched his father perform, that strong chin waggling like a hypnotist's watch…

As with all personalities, the father was blessed with a long and attention-seeking face – hung like a gallery portrait and framed with an abundance of gold and marble hair which swayed when he spoke.

Cotton-blonde eyebrows lay like thatch above sparkling blue eyes – resplendent and magical and untameable blue eyes, twinkling like tumblers of Bombay Sapphire.

A roost for turtle-shell glasses, a majestic pear of a nose stood prominently in the centre of the old man's face like a dictator's monument.

The son's had been toppled in a previous uprising…

And the father dressed more elegantly than his son.

Timelessly. With pungency.

For the attention and appreciation of others.

This morning he modelled a sophisticated tweed jacket and matching formal trousers.

Butter-cream shirt.

Gold watch.

Gold ring.

Knotted strawberry and lime neckerchief the cherry on top.

All in all, a bedazzling patchwork of colours and conflicts.

Yet somehow understated.

At ease.

At one.

At home under the limelight.

And so the father continued playing to his enraptured audience.

An Audience With…

Complete with canned laughter by a crowd long-since deceased…

"And at the BAFTAs, seventy-four, I believe, a certain adolescent with a certain fizzy beverage splashed a certain leading lady I had my eye on.

"Never did get my hands around those famous hips – all thanks to this little bugger!" the old man gleamed, motioning to ruffle his son's hair.

"And to cap it all off," he added with mild yet noticeable bitterness, "that sly Taff she was so enamoured with took home the gong…

"Pah! Not that I minded – plenty of silver in the kitty and wine in the cellar and toys under the tree come Christmas.

"From what I remember we did alright, didn't we lad?"

The son rolled his eyes.

"Can't say the same for the Taff." the father added. "He's renting in Huntingdon, I believe.

"Third floor. One bedroom.

"I wouldn't feel right speaking for her…"

And so the father concluded his eulogy:

"Eheu fugaces labuntur anni.

"Alas, the fleeting years slip by."

The Stanlows were close to tears.

The son was bored to the point of them…

He squinted to the TV, watching the detective stumble drunkenly through the front door of his apartment – in doing so, he tripped over a child's train set, trampling it down to the cogs.

"Now," said the father with raised and appreciative hands, once the Stanlow's incessant plaudits had tempered down. "If you'll permit, let me ask of you, this."

He leant across the table.

The detective collapsed on the staircase.

"Do either of you remember Table for Two?"

The son watched a boy stand crying at the top of the stairs, while his father fell asleep at the foot of them.

Like so many, this had been a difficult episode to endure…

Four

With signed napkins and embellished anecdotes to parade before their neighbours, the Stanlows had finally taken their leave.

Thank fucking Christ…

The son found himself sitting alone at the cafeteria table, resting drowsily on his elbows.

He yawned for the hell of it.

Coughed with discomfort.

Still playing silently on the far wall, the detective show was thick into its second act.

Nobody had yet survived an entire episode…

Through the rain-speckled window beside him, the son cast his tired eyes across the hospital car park:

The car park itself was half full, and entrenched by various wards and surgeries – all had their blinds drawn.

Beyond was a road leading to a duel carriageway.

Beyond that, a large grey retail park, partly obscured behind trees.

And beyond that, some hills.

The son yawned again.

Invigorating stuff…

He patted his inside pocket.

No divertissement to be found there, either…

On a positive note, the rain was easing off. Thinning away. Few were carrying umbrellas from their cars, now.

Alas, by the looks of the approaching front, the downpour was only taking a breather…

Careful not to spill a drop, the father returned to the table, carrying two steaming mugs.

"Still no calls?" he challenged.

"Not since you asked two minutes ago…

"Probably a good thing, mind."

The father didn't reply.

He placed the two mugs on the table.

"I brought you a coffee.

"A large one.

"Since arriving you've acted like you could use it – if only to drown that frog in your throat.

"And warming up." the old man added, sitting himself down. "You're shivering like the hind legs of a whippet."

The son motioned sardonically to the weather outside...

From his jacket pocket the father produced three small milk pots, the type they have in cheap hotels.

He arranged them in a line on the table.

He removed his jacket, straightened his back, and adjusted his cuffs.

Slowly, he peeled back the lid of the first pot.

The son exhaled.

Let the lashing commence...

"It was good of you to come today, David." the father spoke as though initiating a police interview. "To make the time."

The son picked up his coffee.

"Thanks for inviting me..." he replied with considerable sarcasm.

With polygraph eyes examining, the father enquired:

"I expect everything is dandy in your world?"

"I can't complain."

The textbook reply...

"Fixed in a routine and out of trouble?" the old man furthered, adding the milk to his tea.

"A routine, at least." the son answered.

"Occupied?"

"Whenever possible."

"You're eating well?"

"Fresh from the can."

"And you're healthy?"

A sip of coffee.

"I can't complain..."

Eyes down, the father methodically stirred his tea with a plastic stick.

When the contents had stopped spinning, he drank in silence…

The detective show was currently between adverts – retirement homes and offers on litre spirits.

The son thought it wise not to mention either…

"And you?" he eventually offered, sensing his cue to speak. "What have you been up to?"

The father looked straight through him.

"Gardening."

This was the father the son recognised – the only one he'd known since adolescence.

That flourishing and irrepressible enthusiasm with which the old man had garnished the Stanlows had promptly been withdrawn – folded up and hidden away like a costume. Now, in the gated company of his only son, the old man was as hard and impulsive as a gavel…

He put down his tea, and clicked his tongue.

He shook his head disparagingly.

"Brass spoon…"

The second pot of milk was incorporated…

The two men took it in turns to look out of the window – monitoring the scenery as though it could be snatched away at any moment.

Crows with greasy beaks were landing on the roofs of the parked cars, causing a nuisance.

"You look different to when I saw you last." the father assessed of his son, yet his attention all the while fixated on the birds.

"Maybe it was the suit?" the son suggested. "Hadn't worn it in years. Not my style."

"Even in black."

The father's attention remained with the window.

Those birds…

Pecking at their reflections in the wing mirrors…

"Did anyone mind that I couldn't stay after?" the son offered in the form of an apology. "Back in spring. When we last met up.

"I felt off about leaving early."

The old man banged his fist on the window.

It had no effect…

"Your aunt wouldn't have cared." he said.

"Was it a good service?"

The father shrugged.

"Charles seemed to think so. We all agreed it was a very moving departure."

The son swirled his coffee, scraping the base of the mug on the table.

"I wanted to stay longer." he added, eyes down. "But I had to get away.

"Uncle Chuck said he understood.

"He, at least, appreciated my reasons…"

"Like I say," the father determined, "Your aunt, she wouldn't have cared."

A bedraggled parking warden was shooing the birds away.

He was making a poor job of it…

The father shook his head, returning to his original observation.

"No. Something other than your attire, lad.

"A change in your being. A physical transformation."

"Tired, perhaps?" the son considered – a yawn, partly intentional, emphasised his point.

"I haven't been sleeping well. Not for a couple of weeks.

"And four-on, four-off, doesn't help."

The father disregarded this excuse as circumstantial.

"This time of year it's bright all the time, anyway. What difference could the hours make?"

"They take their toll, Pops."

"Not always they didn't – you've always been a creature of the night." the father retorted. "Besides, in your younger days, how were you excusing your proclivity towards hibernation?:

"'I'm a musician, Dad.

"'An Artist. A frontman.

"'We're just wired differently.

"'Not like the rest of you old normies.'"

The impression was uncanny – the whiny voice and irritable mannerisms caricatured yet precise.

Right down to the clenching of the nostrils.

The father chuckled to himself.

"There goes Rock-a-billy David." he reminisced, taking his tea. "'Prick up, pricks! Here's another one you won't like!'"

"I still play."

The father was surprised at his son's bullish admission. Concerned, even.

"I thought you'd given up on all that nonsense a long time ago?"

The son chewed his coffee.

Nonsense…

Fucking nonsense…

"I'd only assumed," the father reinforced, "given your years and as many knock-backs besides, you'd have abandoned that fruitless vocation altogether – left your guitar in the attic and eyeliner in the bin."

A sip.

"Where they belong."

"I dust off the old six-string and tonsils every now and then, when I can spare an evening." the son countered brazenly. "For shits and giggles."

The father didn't approve of his son's language.

Or lifestyle.

"It's good fun." the son clarified, scratching his elbow. "The banter. Catching up with the lads – Andy and Col and sometimes Ian. The boys reunited, back on the prowl, riling the crowds like we used to."

The son cracked a smile, the first in too long.

It caused his bottom lip to split.

"This time of year we'll always take a booking or three. Either end of the country, any time, day or night – a night on the road makes no difference to us."

With the napkin from his pocket, he blotted the droplets of blood from his lips.

"We'll take all the gigs we can handle.

"While we still can…"

"Well, if you think it'll serve you." the father implied as though a warning. "You know my thoughts on the whole business, however."

Indeed he did.

And that made the suffering all the sweeter…

Back to the window – visitors were vacillating between a one or two hours' stay, a fiver versus a tenner, the true value of their time when measured against that of their relatives.

"How is she, anyway?"

"Your mother is herself. Coming and going each day but always with a smile." the father replied, fidgeting with his wedding ring.

It gleamed under the light.

The son could never get over how pristine it was.

"And today's nothing major." the father assured, if only for his own benefit. "Nothing to get worked up over.

"Nothing to worry about.

"It's just…" he said, clearing his throat. "What with everything that's happened these past months, I thought it best that we both…"

Momentarily, the old man fell silent – the foundations of his composure crumbling.

The son moved to speak.

Yet he dithered – and the moment slipped him by…

The father quickly regained himself, and continued.

"You simply being here makes it easier for her. A comfort she could sorely use.

"She often asks after you."

The son admitted to knowing this…

The detective show had finished. A list of names rolled down the screen.

Most were dead.

Now it was time for news and antiques.

"You're travelling back with us tonight?" the father expected.

The son rubbed his neck.

"We'll see how it goes."

The old man pouted.

"I see. Got to scamper home to… what was her name again?

"Nelly? Kelly?"

"Elly." the son said, knowingly.

"Elly…" the father hissed.

The name tasted foul on his lips – like that of a racehorse which had cost him his fortune.

"You and your precious little Elly…"

"She sends her love." the son shot back, forked tongue renewed and 'a lashing.

"Oh I don't doubt that she does." the father grunted. "When did she last not lavish me with such scented pleasantries?

"End of the fiscal year, wasn't it?"

"This morning, actually. She wanted to thank you for the card."

"At least I think she said 'thank'…" the son mocked, tugging his ear lobe. "Too many gigs. Bad for the shells."

"She called you this morning?"

"Yeah. When I was having a puff."

The old man was perturbed by this.

"You talked to her?"

"It's what people do, Pops…"

"For how long?"

"You want the transcript?"

The old man's face reddened.

"How long did you speak with her, David?"

The son slumped back in his chair.

"I don't know. A few minutes." he cared to guess. "Five, give or take."

The father was furious – all apoplectic and fists.

If they weren't in public he would have roared the house down.

"What if the nurses had called?! Did you think of that?

"Something might have happened to your mother!"

"Nothing did happen." the son contested. "And if it did—"

"Check your phone."

"It was five minutes."

"They may have left a message!"

"They haven't!"

Enough! The father had had his fill.

He stretched out his hand.

"Give it here, lad."

"Jesus! I would have fucking noti—"

"I said give it!"

The son pulled out his phone and threw it across the table.

The old man fumbled with it, squeezing its edges like an ape with a brick.

Eventually the screen came to life.

Displayed over an old family photo were the time, date, and today's forecast.

Nothing else.

The son folded his arms.

"See? What did I say?"

The father slid the phone back across the table.

This didn't prove anything.

This wasn't the point...

"Heavier."

"Err?" the son responded, irked as though woken with a flannel.

"That's how you've changed." the father clarified, inspecting his son beneath the rims of his tortoise shell glasses. "I see it now.

"You look heavier."

Finishing his tea in a single gulp and grabbing his jacket, he concluded:

"Mind, you always were a fat baby."

Before the son could get to his feet, the father had already deserted him...

The son returned to the window.

His breath fogged the glass...

In no desire to give chase yet feeling himself obliged to do so, he drained his coffee and left the mug where it landed.

Rising, he collected his phone.

Fucker had chipped the screen...

On leaving the cafeteria, the son tossed his bloodied napkin into a waste bin. He helped himself to a few more from a table.

He also took the opportunity to alleviate some rubbish from his pockets:

A few receipts. Old train tickets.

The wet cigarette box.

He discretely took a glance over his shoulder. Waited for the opportune moment.

A coffee machine vented.

The empty bottle landed in the bin with a thud.

The son disguised it with a cough, and quickly moved on.

Five

Each keeping to their own, both father and son took up their respective positions in the hospital corridor.

Attending.

Expectant.

But never together.

While one man waited on the green plastic bench, the other was inevitably absent.

His seat taken if anyone asked…

The father took the first stint. First watch.

He preferred to. Stipulated so.

Arms folded, he tucked in his knees with polite English repression as another bed-bound patient was squeaked down the tight and congested corridor, double doors and uncertainty awaiting them.

Elsewhere, in the fashion cats roam alleys, the son maundered the wards.

Counting down the hours.

Familiarising himself…

Shit.

The newsagents in the lobby didn't stock cigarettes.

A wanting substitute, the son bagged two cans of coke and made his way outside.

He didn't join the smokers – without a fag to hand he would've felt himself an intruder. Instead he found a bench in a sheltered corner between trees, overlooking the car park.

He sipped his coke while deleting some old text messages, freeing up space.

Emptying his memory.

He spat on the ground – coffee-infused mucus which still lingered at the back of his throat.

He finished his coke.

Located a bin.

Missed on the rim.

Collected and shot again.

Fruitless, but it killed a few minutes...

Back inside, a foreign cleaner was busy mopping the corridor. Ears bunged, music tinny, he hummed the translations to Western hits.

With minimal regret he spilt a container of blue cleaning fluid across the floor.

The father lifted his legs while the spill was mopped away.

He'd dry his shoes later...

The son checked the timetables for buses running to and from the hospital. He took a photo on his phone.

Later he walked a lap around the outskirts of the main building, hugging the walls to keep dry of the rain.

He nosed onto a few wards – most had their curtains drawn, but some showed signs of life.

Or at least something resembling it...

Pale, poultry-coloured old ladies were having oxygen masks wrapped across their faces.

The disabled were struggling through a yoga routine.

Bald and disconsolate chemo patients sat lifeless in rows – like boxes of eggs, the son considered.

They looked fitter than he did.

Fitter than he felt.

According to his phone, his second lap was a minute slower.

The third slower still.

The forth resulted in a stripping cough, flogging pain – one which had kept him awake for several nights.

On the way back he purchased a packet of lozenges.

"They sell The Telegraph downstairs." he informed his father.

The old man acknowledged this plainly.

"Surprising, their leanings considered..."

"Comes with free mints."

"Is that so?"

"While stocks last."

The father moved his jacket from the seat beside him.

The son sat down in its place.

"Any news?" he asked, offering a lozenge.

The father shook his head.

"Messages?" he himself enquired.

"Why would there be?" was the obvious response.

Another bed was wheeled down the corridor, plastic sacks of fluid surrounding it like blimps.

"What happened to your shoes?" the son asked, popping a lozenge.

"Accident."

A pause.

"Well… don't feel too embarrassed." the son consoled in a tender, albeit mocking voice.

He patted his father's knee.

"It can't be helped. As we get older these things are bound to hap—"

"Grow up, David."

The son cracked open his second can, sniggering conceitedly to himself.

He took a slug, still sniggering.

He gagged on his lozenge…

The father made a point of stretching. He stood and collected his jacket.

"Keep my place."

This directive the son obeyed until the father returned twenty-minutes later, newspaper tucked under arm.

"A&E's quiet." he noted. "Must be too early for the winos."

He removed the empty can from the bench and sat down.

As though on a see-saw, the son got up.

"I'm going for a piss."

The father popped a mint, and opened the paper…

And so this routine of cordial absence ran its course for the next few hours, both men coming and going without acknowledgement as though actors passing in the wings between scenes.

Only nodding out of professional courtesy.

***

When the son returned from another prolonged excursion he found his father in conference with a nurse.

When the discussion was concluded, the father thanked her.

He even touched her arm.

The old man seemed brighter. Rejuvenated. Elevated by a renewed buoyancy. He practically skipped across the corridor towards his son, urgent to share the news.

"Your mother's out of surgery!" he beamed, slapping the rolled newspaper against his open palm. "Everything went like clockwork. Could not have gone better, they say."

"That's great." the son reciprocated, being careful not to crack his lips again. "Is she awake?"

"Not for a while yet. They say she'll be away with the fairies for a good couple of hours. Those drugs must pack a wallop!"

The son could imagine so.

"But we'll be able to see her later this afternoon." the father added. "Allow her time to get her head together, poor thing."

The old man looked to the clock on the wall as though the rising sun.

He patted the newspaper again.

"Well now," he announced, "I'd say it's time we found ourselves some lunch."

Six

The father was adamant. "Mark my words, lad – this rain'll restart soon's we're heading back." he asserted with a disdainful look to the clouds, one leg already inside the car.

This the son refuted – such was the present outbreak of radiant sunshine he'd prefer they walked the short distance to the retail park, rather than the old man waste time driving.

But the father was adamant.

Adamant.

Thus the matter was settled.

"Typical British weather." he grunted with a slipping of gears.

"A bitch that can never be trusted."

"That's the spirit, Pops…"

The son climbed into the car moments before it pulled away, slamming the passenger door behind him.

Craving the breeze, he wound down his side window.

The father leant across and wound it back up.

***

Just as expected…

Lunchtime traffic as immovable as the concrete being jackhammered beside it.

From the passenger seat, the son looked over his father's head.

He could practically spit on the retail park from here…

"Mark my words…" the old man reiterated, shuffling endlessly through commercial radio stations for a traffic report, creating surreal avant-garde music with the dial. "You'll thank me later."

"Later. Exactly…"

The son had always considered himself a miscreant when riding in his father's car.

Ill fitting. Dirty. Stig of the Dump squatting in a palace.

Every surface he touched left a fingerprint akin to a lesion.

When he adjusted himself, the upholstery squeaked as though offended or maimed.

The seatbelt, he was certain, had intentions on choking him…

The son didn't know the make of his father's car – even as a boy he had never cared about such superficial trivialities. All he knew was that it was painted a tawny gold, furnished with pine, and maintained impeccably by its devoted chaperone.

A servant to pride, the father would never contemplate treating his car in a manner more assertive than consummate delicacy. When undertaking a three-point turn, for example, he refused to rotate the steering wheel while the vehicle was stationary.

It would take years off the tyres.

Years, David.

The son had never learned to drive…

Up ahead, the lights turned green.

The father took his chance and bolted – but a colourless eurobox pulled out injudiciously.

The old man braked. Gesticulated. Slammed his palm against the horn.

With immediate repentance he buffed his hand print from the steering wheel with his sleeve.

The oils might stain the brass…

The son adjusted himself again.

With ignominy, the leather cried out.

This car…

This fucking car…

The car the old man had brought with his first major pay cheque.

The car which had delivered the newborn son home.

Yet, in all the years and all the hours and all the miles he'd spent barricaded in this bastard box on wheels, the son was unable to recall the rear seats ever being occupied.

***

Pandering to the clutch as one would a floozy, the father eased the car into position, undertaking two attempts before halting precisely parallel in the emptiest and furthermost corner of the retail park.

The son squinted – as though Saharan apparitions, he could faintly distinguish the outlines of shops in the far distance.

"We may as well have walked…"

"I thought we might get ourselves some butties." the father proposed, climbing out and gently closing the driver's door behind him.

He ensured it was locked.

"There's a superstore across the way. Meal deals. Should be inexpensive."

And heaving this time of day, the son imagined, unbuttoning his jacket.

He wriggled from the car and cricked his neck.

His forehead was already beginning to glaze.

"Do you want, or need, to pick up anything?" the father asked while inspecting the tyres. "Any essentials for the days ahead?"

"As we're here." the son agreed wearily. "I could do with a few top-ups for the fridge. Refreshments and the like."

The father nodded. Oblivious to the gleaming sunshine, he instructed:

"You can stick it all in the boot once we're done.

"Frozens won't go off. Not in this climate."

The old man checked the driver's door a final time, the same routine passenger side, then onwards towards the superstore.

The son trailed a few paces behind, tallying the credits in his wallet…

The retail park housed a variety of outlets – everyday franchises for the everyday consumer. There was a cinema. A pet store. A clothing warehouse. A DIY centre. A bistro. And other shops and distractions usually embedded on the high street.

But most predominantly there stood a supermarket – attracting crowds comparable to the Kaaba, it was the shape of a magnet and the size of an aircraft hanger.

Keeping to the pavement which linked the attractions, the two men continued their long pilgrimage towards it.

Walking side by side. Matching cavalier struts.

The father always leading marginally.

He walked with a slight stoop, the son noticed of his father's comportment – a spine curved like the stalk of a pear.

He ambled briskly, give him his due – yet attentively.

Deliberately.

The hands clasped at his back were perhaps a means to equalise ballast? the son wondered.

Or to conceal discomfort?

Regardless, the father still led the way. Monty on the march. The son his loyal battalion.

Orderly.

Obedient.

Forever on the cusp of mutiny…

The father sniffed the air, catching a hearty aroma which vented from the kitchens of a small nearby gastropub.

"Beef." he inhaled wantingly, a succulence to each individual word.

"Hot, English, Roast, Beef."

Tearing himself away from a shop window displaying cots, the son himself took the air.

His sinuses may well have been scorched, yet still he identified the whiff of:

"Dripping."

"No mistaking it." the father confirmed, scanning the gastropub's blackboard menu. "Never did me any harm."

The place looked reasonably quiet, both men agreed.

And reasonably priced.

Yet nothing was ventured – and so the expedition pressed on…

Further along the way, the pair fell under the shadow of a large bowling alley.

Bassy music, akin to industrial machinery requiring maintenance, pounded heavily.

Both men winced. Not their type of genre. No structure or form.

Too modern – this they could both agree on.

A mass of neon-fringed teenagers burst from the centre's doors and began laughing hysterically.

They were mostly girls. Top-heavy teens carrying phones as big as bricks.

As they flounced off in a fit of giggles, a boy with frosty hair hopped longingly in pursuit, one trainer missing.

"School must be out for the week." the father suggested, stepping aside gentlemanly for the fleeing girls.

The group looked back at him, momentarily distracted. In doing so they ran out in front of an oncoming car. Much honking and merriment ensued.

"The last break until the summer stretch." the son gathered.

"Is that so?"

"I'd guess."

"Elly tell you that?" the father commented.

The son ignored him.

***

Inside the supermarket, the father struggled to separate the last two available shopping baskets, which had seemingly become fused together.

Eventually, begrudgingly, he accepted his son's assistance.

On the father's count, each man grabbed a basket, and pulled.

Wrestled.

Tugged.

Hungry dogs fighting over a ribcage.

With a sudden snap the baskets separated.

The son's had surrendered its handle…

Great. Fine. Whatever. He'd go find a trolley.

An inspection of the watch.

"We'll meet back here in, shall we agree, twenty minutes?" the father made it plain.

To this the son conceded.

"You got a quid?" he asked, rummaging through his jacket. "For the trolley."

Smirking, the old man slipped his son a penny wrapped in cellotape.

"The fuck is this?"

"Cunning, my lad." the father replied, tapping his temple.

"And don't worry about removing it from the trolley after you're done." he added, heading off into the store. "I've got plenty more where that came from."

Shaking his head in bewilderment, the son abandoned his basket and trudged outside.

Just as the father had prophesied, the clouds were regrouping forebodingly…

Kin

***

Aisle seven, and distraction music was interrupted by a tyrannical announcement:

'All available staff must report to the tills! All available staff must report to the tills!'

Hurrying. Harrying. Half empty pallets abandoned mid-aisle.

And then the music restarted.

Like a fucking death camp...

The son had always despised megastores.

Depressing places. Fly paper for the penniless.

Every aspect of these colosseums to capitalism drained his spirit as though blood syphoned from his wrists – the boardroom conceived and meeting table agreed and management team implemented monotonousness masquerading as impromptu.

The music aisle irked him the most:

Greatest hits. Compilations. An artist's life's work stacked and racked.

All for 99p a disc.

The son watched a woman grab a handful of Best Ofs and toss them into her basket with all the consideration afforded empty wrappers.

The royalties would barely amount to a penny...

The music stopped again.

'Clean up on aisle six! Clean up on aisle six!'

The son looked down at his trolley's two lonely incumbents – a jar of fish paste and a tube of Pringles.

Between them lay a deep, barren trench.

Much deeper than there would have been with a basket...

For what the son desperately needed, needed concealing...

And so he began by picking up the typicals. The basics.

Bread. Milk. Butter. Cheese.

Biscuits. Ham. Coffee. A chicken.

A half-wheel of misshapen quiche from the reduced section – an excuse for lunch.

Fags he'd get on the way out.

Elly had mentioned something about bean sprouts – a recipe a friend had posted after gapping in Japan.

Broad beans were on offer.

Sounded close enough.

He grabbed two packets.

Make that three.

Yet still there was too much open space…

The son scoured the aisles, Supermarket Sweep-style.

Bag upon bag of bargain multibuys were ransacked from the freezers – chips and meats and nuggets and veg.

And to top it all off, a proverbial duvet for the bed, the biggest variety pack of crisps he could carry.

Now he had cover.

Now the trolley was prepared.

Wheeling it gingerly, the son arrived at the final aisle in the store – his intended destination all along:

Beers, Wines & Spirits…

He took a cursory, cautionary glance to both ends of the aisle.

A listen for footsteps approaching the bedroom door.

In a single movement, without stopping, the son grabbed by the neck a 35cl bottle of his dependable brand:

Gold crest. Green glass.

Pocket size…

A screech, startling.

"Look, it's him! Him!"

The son's heart pounded – an attack coming on.

In a flounder he almost dropped the bottle, catching and coddling it against his chest as though an infant.

Like a squirrel with a nut, the son buried the bottle beneath the other groceries in his trolley while laughter overflowed from the opposite aisle – churlish squeals like a parade of fluffy hatchlings.

Followed by the curdling boom of a duplicitous old fox:

"Indeed! Tis I! The great one and only!

"Do not let me distract you again, my pretties!"

The son caught his breath.

Pops…

As he rounded the corner onto the confectionery aisle, the son found his father to be the centre of attention, surrounded as he was by a gaggle of young girls.

He recognised them as the same girls whom had earlier exploded from the bowling alley – tarts in tight white jeans with crop-tops and dyed hair, hopping and skipping around the father's ankles as though he were a maypole.

They insisted on selfies – copious gawps framed in at a time.

Arms around the waist and pecks on the cheek.

Mummy's lipstick smudged across the father's blooded jowls.

And of course the old man was acting the cornered and defenceless grandparent to aplomb, milking the adulation for every drop it was worth…

Phones brimmed with intermittent posterity, the girls eventually moved on, energy drinks and Nutella under their arms.

The father waved them off, their blown kisses caught and preserved for later.

The son approached from behind. Coughed.

"Young admirers of mine." the father explained with neither guilt nor embarrassment – only swollen pride.

"They've seen me in some serial or other.

"I can't recall which.

"That fantasy thing with the dragons, perhaps?"

"Weren't you killed off?"

No reply. Perhaps the old man hadn't heard him?..

The most buxom of the girls peeked around the corner of the aisle. Before vanishing again, she flashed the father a glossy, cherry lips pout.

The father winked back.

His better winks.

"Wandsworth quail." the son warned, shaking his head in disapproval. "Fifteen straight for fifteen bait."

The father frowned, picking up his basket.

"If you say so, David.

"You're quite the graduate regarding such matters."

The son swung his trolley around.

"And you're the veteran, Pops."

The father ignored him.

***

"Christ almighty! Didn't I say this would happen."

A thud.

"Didn't I just tell you, lad."

Another.

"Typical." the old man bemoaned, palms cupped upwards like scales.

"Just typical…"

"I told you more rain was forecast, didn't I?"

"You might have mentioned it…"

And to make matters worse, the two men's shopping was getting wetter by the moment, many a plastic bag dotted with moisture as though perspiring.

As a result, they were loaded into the back of the father's car with unceremonious haste.

This task the son found himself undertaking alone…

"No really…" he muttered under spiteful breath, ducking back and forth under the boot lid. "Please, I'll manage… I've carried them this far."

Oblivious, the father looked to the clouds as though trying to spot a leak in the ceiling.

"Typical. Just typical." he muttered again.

"A bloody bitch…"

He was holding two incarcerated triangles of damp, rubbery sandwich.

Egg – a syllable for each yolk.

The rain caused the labels to peel.

"I'd planned on enjoying these outside – hardly the weather, now."

"Never is." the son replied, two bags deposited with a thud.

"You could always eat them in the car." he teased, winding his father on.

Heresy!

"With these crumbs? I've just had the leather buffed!

"And the bread's seeded."

"Seeded, you say?.."

"Sodden!" the father continued. "Thing'll be nothing but mush the time I've finished."

"Time you're finished I'll be fuck'in mush…"

While the old man grieved, the son took the opportunity to slip the bottle into his jacket pocket.

"What luncheon did you procure for yourself?" the father grumbled.

Another thud.

"Lump of old quiche."

"Sounds nourishing…

"Protein. Important…

"Anything else, to make a meal of it?"

A great sack of crisps was waved over the boot lid.

"We won't starve, then."

"Help yourself." the son offered. "Might firm-up your butty."

The father inspected said butty:

It looked soggy and sad…

"I don't even like rye." he stated, lost to grief.

"Fuck me…"the son hissed to himself. "Enough to turn anyone to drink…"

A rustling from the crisps masked an impatient breaking of the cap.

The resulting swig was swift, secretive—

And desperately needed.

The father sniffed the air, nostrils wide.

"You know what I smell, lad?"

The son swallowed. Almost choked.

"What?" he coughed.

"That gastropub over the way… the one we passed earlier…"

"Oh, right. Yeah." the son exhaled, tucking the bottle back into his coat and discretely wiping his mouth. "Smelt like dripping."

The father paused for a moment.

Contemplated.

He ambled over to the boot.

"Perhaps…"

He scratched his chin.

"She'll be a while, they said.

"And there haven't been any messages, have there?"

The son shook his head, still collecting and depositing the bags, crane-like.

A taking of the air.

"No calls?"

"No."

"No texts?"

"Nout."

An exhale.

Humming.

Another scratch of the chin.

The son next expected the sending up of a flair.

Or the awarding of an Oscar…

"You're quite sure?" the old man further sought. "No messages?"

"Because I'm told the reception in those supermarkets is—"

"No messages, Pops!"

The father turned again to the gastropub – steam was rising from the aluminium chimneys at its rear, dispelling the rain.

Which was beginning to worsen…

The father looked down at his sandwich.

Then back to his son.

"Wouldn't be the worst idea, would it, lad?"

The son rubbed circulation back into his plastic-spliced fingers.

The last two bags were deposited, the lid slammed, and the trolley kicked away.

And thus, the matter was settled.

Seven

Closing the doors of the gastropub behind them, the father and the son wiped their shoes on the welcome mat, and shook the rain from their sleeves.

Spirit levels for the bar, a pair of unshaven old men briefly looked up from their halves to inspect the newcomers, before returning to their shared pencilling of the Racing Post.

Over wine, four lunching accountants sunk back into their croutons.

Practically muted, a reproduction jukebox cycled mp3s from the corner...

The gastropub itself was unnamed – it only bore the branding of its national chain. Yet both father and son found it to be a charming little cubbyhole.

A working class atmosphere.

Elbows on tables.

Hot wedges served in novelty tin buckets.

Strictly no children.

If the food was decent and the quietude retained across the day, both men could imagine themselves frequenting regularly.

Albeit with different partners.

Or preferably alone...

Noses hoisted, they embraced the welcoming aroma.

The aroma of blushing meat.

Honey-glazed vegetables.

"And God's own dripping!"

What more could two men ask for?

A heaving portion, for one...

The father had his heart set on the House Special – Roast beef with Yorkshire puddings, potatoes, peas, carrots, parsnips, stuffing, onions, sausages and gravy. Xtra Large for an extra pound, encouraged the bar-side placard.

"With a second dollop of the horseradish sauce!" the father announced, unbuttoning his jacket.

The son would have the same.

The father suggested a table in the corner against the wall.

The son would keep his seat.

"Drink?" the old man offered, making the obligatory hand gesture. "Included in the deal.

"I'm sticking with water – lemon, sparkling, and lashings of ice."

He was driving.

In a moment of absent-mindedness, the son admitted that he could "murder a pint."

It sounded like a confession – an admittance of guilt.

He looked to his father, all Bambi double-blinks and ghee.

"As we're here, you know…

"If you're paying?"

The old man signalled nothing. He reached for his wallet.

"Hey, what's the harm? Who's to say I shouldn't have a drink?" the son quarrelled.

Each excuse a shovel deeper…

"Look, they've got prize winning ales on offer.

"Local brews.

"So the poster says…

"And it's past lunchtime,

"And you're happy to drive,

"And it's gonna be a big meal, so…"

"You're a grown man, David – you don't have to ask for my consent.

"You're not on trial."

It always felt like it…

While the father headed for the bar to do the honours with additional and politely received patter, the son removed his leather jacket and flung it over the back of his chair.

In his haste he did so carelessly.

The bottle in his inside pocket sounded against the wooden banister – a midnight knocking at the window.

To the son's relief, the father hadn't noticed – he was busy asking the odds, lending his pen.

The son quickly adjusted the coat's hang. Folded it twice over. Hung it to one side.

He put his phone on the table, and sat down.

An alleviating exhale tickled loose a cough...

The table was constructed from weathered wooden planks like an old keg – it wobbled as the son slid his knees beneath it. The two chairs at either side were imitation oak, and bound with burgundy leather, distressed at the seams both intentionally and through wear.

Beside the table stood a large plant in a terracotta pot, its crown roughly the height of a child. The leaves of the plant were thick and rubbery – probably plastic, the son imagined.

In the pot, surrounding the plant's trunk, were dozens of little white pebbles – also plastic.

On the surrounding brick walls, displayed with all the artistry of safety notices, hung digitally faded posters and reproduction oil paintings.

The frames were ornate. Gold.

And, unsurprisingly, plastic.

There was also a large mirror, in which, framed as though a mugshot, the son caught sight of his reflection:

As pale and as weathered as a washed up whale...

Skinny fat. An over-filled chipolata ready to pop its casing...

And that fucking nose... red, chapped and dripping, the father's intentions having tenderised it.

Repulsed, the son adjusted his seat and busied himself with the paintings...

Most were of abstract bottles and the like.

Clip art brewing apparatus in silhouette.

Nondescript fruit in a cubist parody.

All very much of a muchness.

But one painting across the way caught the son's eye – despite being in no way an authority or connoisseur of art, he found himself drawn to this single piece:

A broad painting. Resounding.

It depicted two overlapping spirit bottles on a fiery yellow canvas.

One bottle was predominant.

Central.

Magenta.

The second was a bit astride, off kilter, left, beneath the first and slightly smaller and celery green.

Where the two bottles overlapped there manifested a void of blank, barren canvas.

The son removed his tinted glasses, so as to better read the inscription at the painting's base.

'Kin'.

"I don't see how you can wear those things indoors." stated the returning father, depositing the drinks on the slate coasters provided. "They make you look like a blind beggar."

Blinking the moisture away, the son pulled a finger across his left eye and put the glasses in question back on.

"They're in fashion."

"Are they now?"

"Yeah. Trending."

The old man wasn't convinced.

Chewing a mint, he hung his jacket over his seat, and sat down.

"Are all the 'kids' wearing them these days? Like some bohemian Day of the Triffids?"

The son leant forward and collected his pint.

"Nah. These days I hear they're more into neckerchiefs with pretty little flowers on."

The father adjusted said neckerchief – he ensured both ends were of equal length.

"Well," he mused, "I congratulate today's generation on their impeccable taste."

The son allowed a chuckle to crack his lips.

As did the father. An off-guard twinkle.

A spark escaping the kiln.

"Sainted Lanc."

The son emoted that he didn't understand.

"Floral and hay-like with a hint of thyme." the father explained, pointing to the marigold pint at his son's lips. "I'm told it complements the beef."

"Nice." the son duly confirmed with a second taste. "Hay… yeah…"

"Definitely hay…"

The father smirked – a derisive expression.

"You should have gotten one for yourself." the son couldn't help but riposte.

The old man shook his head. He'd stick to his water.

He was driving…

"Little tip." he offered via demonstration. "Tuck your pinkie under your pint. That way there's no risk of dropping it when your grip gets a little… relaxed."

"Learnt from experience?" the son jabbed.

"Larry." the old man winked. "One of the many tricks he imparted."

There was a small wooden dish of pork scratchings on the table. The son nibbled a few and offered the dish to his father.

"Not right now, if you mind.

"Once I start I'll never stop."

The son himself didn't need a second invitation – he dove in all the deeper.

"Did they say how long the roasts are gonna take?" he asked, mid-crunch.

They hadn't – yet, for some reason only known to himself, the father consulted his watch all the same.

"Ten or so minutes, I'd presume.

"Give or take."

"Could well be longer for the roasties?"

"Perhaps." the father considered.

Another crunch.

"And veg can't be hurried."

"Hmm…"

The son offered the scratchings again.

The father succumbed.

But just the one.

The largest from the top.

Well, as two were stuck together…

***

The son's phone buzzed like a hornet.

The old man almost choked on his scratching.

"Relax. It's not them over the road." the son assured, checking the phone. "It's a…

"Nuisance text…"

A swipe of the screen. Guarded.

"Some automated bot – a computer asking if I have PPI or some shit."

He put the phone back down on the table.

It buzzed again as though abandoned. A whining bitch begging to be let in.

"Fucking nuisance…"

Twenty turgid minutes had come and gone.

The son's pint was two thirds of the way down.

And a look over his shoulder confirmed that the heralded roasts showed no signs of arriving…

The father checked his wristwatch – like a wind-up manakin, he'd been doing so every other minute.

"That thing tell you the gas mark as well?" the son derided.

Without glancing up, the father replied:

"If I had wanted any cheek, David, I would have ordered the pork."

The son saluted his father's comeback with a raising of his pint – it was the first time the old man had spoken since starting on the scratchings.

In the meantime, the son would have another for himself.

While there were any left…

"You always did make a habit of eating before meals." the father recalled.

"Look who's talking…" the son chewed, tonguing the crispy fat from between his teeth.

"Every night without fail." the father continued, fingers laced. "I'd have your supper ready and waiting on the table and you'd be up in your room stuffing yourself silly on toffees and the like."

"Had to." the son replied, arms folded snugly across his paunch. "Considering the meagre portions you served up I'm surprised I didn't waste away to nothing."

"Come now David, you were well nourished."

"For a prisoner of war…"

"You never went hungry." the father asserted. "And I did my damnedest to ensure that you were never left wanting for anything else."

"Alright, I hear you, Pops." the son withdrew.

He took another scratching.

Between thumb and finger he separated the crackling from the flesh.

"But it would have been nice not to have seen the bottom of my plate before I'd started eating." he added as a caveat. "That's all I'm saying."

He flicked the scratching into the air and caught it in his mouth.

"And it would have been nice, just for one dinner, not to have eaten it alone."

The father peered down at his glass – a slice of lemon bobbed on the water's surface under a preserver of bubbles.

"Those were the hours the studio required us to work, lad.

"I, like the crew, never much cared for them…

"Night shoots." the old man sighed, rubbing his eyes. "On location. Out under the stars. The cold made the cameras turn more slowly. The lines harder to read."

He rotated his glass as though screwing in a light-bulb.

"But of course, Auntie had the Corporation's ratings to consider – if cops and robbers were pulling in the viewers on the other side, then we had to do the same.

"I was relieved when they killed me off after the seventh season." the old man stated. "I can't tell you how wearing those scripts had become.

"Works of the Bard, they were not…"

"You always came home in good spirits." the son scoffed, eyebrows cocked. "Merry at worst, I'd say…

"But, hey, whatever pays the rent, right?" he smirked with a spit of the facetious, reaching for his pint. "Magnums and second homes and monthly services didn't pay for themselves."

"Nor did boarding schools." the father pointed, sternly.

"Regardless of the pupil's immediate expulsion…"

A waitress in a black polo shirt approached the pair's table, arms laden with two heaving plates.

In silence, both men picked up their cutlery.

The waitress passed.

She returned a few seconds later, arms empty.

Both men withdrew their knives.

Yet kept them at arm's reach…

The son pushed back his chair and stood up. He downed what remained of his pint – it was mainly foam. Bitter and gassy.

The father had barely touched his water.

"My round, is it?" the son asked vindictively, setting his glass down.

The father waved him away.

"I can endure." he said, looking to the mirror.

There was no queue at the bar – nor was their anyone behind it.

As such, the son perched on a stool, held a tenner between his fingers, and waited.

If he was going to endure, he may as well do so alone.

Eight

Alone at the table, the father sipped his water.

Despite the slice of lemon, it tasted of nothing.

Nothing.

Lancashire rain had more bloody flavour than this…

He turned around in his seat, checking over his shoulder – the lad was still sulking at the bar, shoulders slumped and attention inwards.

Quick as a thief, the old man swiped a couple of pork scratchings from the bowl and swallowed them down.

He recomposed the remaining morsels so their quantity appeared more plentiful.

Then he ate a couple more…

Yet they only made him thirstier.

And the water taste blander…

He checked his watch.

Toyed with his wedding ring.

Licked the salt from his lips.

He remembered the mints in his pocket – complementary with the paper.

Maybe he'd have one?

No. They'd spoil the meal.

And besides, he'd already had some earlier.

As a precaution…

Hanging slovenly from the seat opposite, was the son's coat.

Never did clean up after himself, that one…

Along with his phone, which buzzed routinely, the old man noted that the lad had also neglected to return his empty glass…

Lip stains smudged its rim.

Fingerprints crowded the base like tally marks.

A glacier of white foam trickled down the inside of the bowl.

The father watched it. Tracked it.

Could taste it…

From the corner of his eye he noticed a waitress approach.

In readiness he moved the glass to one side.

As before, the waitress passed by.

He moved the glass back.

His fingers lingered on its cusp…

As though snapping a restraint, the father pulled his hand away and quickly wiped it on his trousers.

Yet the smell of cheap ale still lingered under his nails…

He turned around again.

It appeared the son hadn't ordered yet.

And, regardless of his motives, he had offered…

Perhaps?..

No!

He was driving.

And besides, the old man reminded himself that he no longer needed the grease – the lubrication of alcohol.

The buzz of performing was satisfaction enough – the aroma of an expectant crowd far sweeter than any mere cocktail.

Of this the father was adamant.

Adamant!

Acting was his first love.

His passion. His tipple.

Only these days, however, the well of substitution was fast drying up…

He may not picture himself so, but the father was an elderly man.

Fit for his age, he would argue.

As lean and vivacious as a champion greyhound.

And just as handsome!

Not in a classical sense, he'd accept – more cavalier than titillating. Oak-aged brandy as opposed to a shot.

Yet his was a recognisable face.

Iconic, some might say.

Only these days, however, a portrait etched with heritage was worthless when priced against a more marketable emoji. The new breed of upstarts, the sanctimonious hypocrites, were pushing the old man aside – forcing him out of circulation like a shilling.

He had to face it – the roll call for men in their eighties was fast becoming a whisper…

However, this boy done good would not go quietly into that fair night – not while there was still work to be contested.

Be it only the crumbs from the highchair…

Roles as Wizards and Kings and Grandfathers and Dukes – these were the father's bread and butter.

If those were taken, radio was a regular income and voice-work an honest day's pay.

And you got to sit down…

And there was still his beloved theatre, the intoxicating platform on which he had first discovered his calling.

Although it wasn't the same these days, not now that they permitted that unholy microphone – the whipper-snappers were incapable of projecting into the gods.

How dear Larry must be spinning in his grave…

Reality TV?

He'd been asked, offered.

One time, tempted…

But out of the question.

And the House and the Jungle could get stuffed.

The dancefloor especially. No chance of catching him in sequin!

Writing occupied his nights.

£20-a-photo sci-fi conventions massaged the ego.

And the royalties of the golden years ensured that the house remained warm until Spring.

Settlements notwithstanding…

But yes, after all these years, the old man thanked himself lucky that there was still work to be had.

Still roles. Still parts.

But not leads.

Never leads…

As a climber forever seeks the highest peak while dreaming of former ascents, stardom was what the old man craved.

To be big again.

Centre stage.

Stratospheric.

A god!

Naturally, he'd never confess to this ambition. Not to anyone.

Let alone his son…

To do so would be an insult to the craft. Such repugnant arrogance and self-important me-me-meing were unbecoming of a figure such as David Atherton.

David Atherton M.B.E. – never let them forget that!

Her Majesty had adored his Othello.

She had whispered so…

And her children and their children had recognised him from that space movie. That famous one. From a long time ago in a galaxy far far away.

Or however it went…

Redoubtably, the father was a man of repute.

A gentleman of legacy, integrity and class – of which their was no modern equivalent.

Yet, as of today, he was just an old man that nobody wanted to hire.

With a son he barely recognised.

And a wife laying in the hospital…

Hospitals…

Whatever the outcome, they always took something from you:

A career to indulge.

A family to cherish.

A belly overflowing with pride.

And then, after all the screams and all the blood and all the tears, they tore it out of you. Stripped you. Left you gutted and hollow and divorced of everything that gave your life meaning.

Leaving behind a hole that would never be filled…

The father sniffed his fingers again.

The son was still at the bar.

He hadn't ordered yet.

And he had offered…

Nine

The son remained waiting at the bar, yawning, dog-tired – there were only so many red-ringed pages of the Racing Post he could leaf before becoming drowsy...

What was the point in gambling? he bemoaned.

Win or lose, hard-up or flushed, you weren't even left with a hangover.

Sometimes that was the best part – a hard-earned battle scar as proof of an eventful night.

At least it gave you something to rally against, a reason to get out of bed – if only to chase the hair of the dog.

A little Bourbon on your Cornflakes, as Richards had once prescribed.

Gambling. Pah! Easy come, easy go. It was only money, the son figured.

And he'd pissed away plenty of that in his day...

"How can I fix you?" came a sudden voice with all the awakening of a cockerel's crow.

The son floundered, lost momentarily to his own internal declarations...

A girl behind the bar smiled patiently – a millennial composition of hazelnut and freckles.

"What'll it be?" she again asked.

"Eh..." the son stuttered, "I'll have another of those... Sacred... Tainted?.."

"Sainted." the girl corrected with a heartening smirk. "Our best seller, The Sainted Lanc."

The son nodded – a fetching smile.

"Sounds about right."

Right he was – the girl eagerly wiped dry her hands on her black polo shirt, and began pulling the son's pint.

Her bandy arms were slick with rain, he noticed – her bramble-vine tattoos appearing moistened with dew. Droplets clung to her eyelashes and nose piercing, and from the tips of her candy-accented hair.

And from the looks of it, although he wasn't, it must be perky outside…

"Don't tell anyone." she whispered, leaning in over the bar, "But it makes no difference what you order. It's all from the same barrel."

"Is that right?" the son questioned, playing along.

"Yep. Trade secret."

She flicked a damp purple extension behind her ear.

"But no one ever notices – goes down their necks all the same."

"And comes out the same as well, eh?"

"Don't I know it." the girl acknowledged, topping off the pint and placing it on the bar.

The son thanked her, sipping the overfill.

He was relieved his previous remark hadn't been taken the wrong way…

"Are you visiting someone over the way?" the girl enquired – professional repartee.

"That obvious?" the son replied, folding his arms on the bar.

"Our main source of clientele." the girl smiled, handing back his change. "It's coming up on visiting hours. And you get to recognise the familiar traits after a while."

"And what are my traits?" the son goaded.

The girl rubbed her lips – studious and inquisitive, brown eyes all considering.

"Well," she regarded, "My highly trained senses tell me you're visiting a relative."

The son admitted this to be true.

"A close relative." the girl added. "Immediate family…

"Your mother – that would be my expert intuition."

Although impressed, the son was a little unsettled by the girl's accuracy.

"Nine out of ten, Sherlock."

"What did I miss?" the girl asked.

"Not much. Just the finer details, truth be told…"

"Perhaps I should have added that her procedure was a success, and she'll be awake later this afternoon?"

The son was shocked.

"How the fuck did you?—"

The girl burst out laughing.

"Let's just say I had a little inside information…" she admitted to the son, pointing over his shoulder. "From an old grey dicky bird."

The son now understood.

"My old man's been jabbering, has he?"

The girl nodded, jokingly rubbing her ear.

"Yeah," the son concurred. "He's always got a tale or two to share…"

Whether anyone wanted to hear it or not…

"You both look alike." the girl considered. "Share a roundness. Manly chins.

"You'll age well." she complimented of the son's looks.

"Nice of you to say so." he replied perkily.

"I only say that because your dad looks good for his age – must be a family characteristic."

"One of many I inherited from him."

Whether he liked it or not…

"Your hair's not as thick, though."

"Mother's side." the son confessed.

"And your nose is a bit crooked."

"Father's…"

"And don't take this the wrong way," the girl added. "But…"

She paused, considering the execution of her next observation carefully.

"Go on – you can say it." the son prompted, confident in the thickness of his skin. "I know what you're thinking:

"I'm a bit on the heavier side." he acknowledged, patting his jelly belly.

"It's not that." the girl said.

She leant in, elbows on the bar.

The son's heart fluttered at the scent of her perfume.

"It's your eyes." she said in a whisper.

"They're the saddest I've ever seen…"

The son couldn't bring himself to respond.

Yet, he could agree…

"Oi! Lay-by!" came a guttural interruption – a plague of workmen at the opposite end of the bar.

"When you're about done! We're dying of thirst over here!

"Two Lancs, two Barns, two Evergreens, and a Night Owl." the most boisterous of the clan made clear to all in attendance. "And don't hold back the next wave, neither!"

Pulling herself away, the girl knelt behind the pumps and did as instructed. She flashed the son a discrete and unbecoming gesture of disapproval – tongue in cheek and pumping fist suggestive of what else the workers could go stick down their throats.

The son masked a grin, and left a few pieces of silver on the bar…

On returning to his table, the son was forced to pass between the group of workers. He had no alternative – as though cutting across a field of bulls, he moved quickly, cupping the top of his pint as he squeezed through the herd.

"Lads…"

Armpit to armpit, they didn't make his progress straightforward.

Words were muttered. Intimations. Innuendos. Knowing looks which tormented the son all the way back to the table.

"Made some new friends?" the father asked, busy eyeing daggers at the louts…

He'd been doing so ever since they'd arrived – seven through the door at once, the handle smashed into the wall, their opening utterances of magniloquence being "Fuck!" amongst others.

Sweaty men. Dirty men.

Fluorescent vests over football shirts.

Distended guts and mono brows and flat, hollow heads.

Within seconds of entering the gastropub they had installed themselves at the very top of the pecking order. The dominant predators. Belching gorillas beating their chests.

Had they not been dehydrated, the father could well imagine them marking their territory with strings of yellow piss…

"Hard to believe," he sneered, turning back to his son. "All that labouring and they're still as fat as pigs…"

"Come on Eileen?" came a deafening oink from beside the jukebox.

"Life is a Rollercoaster?

"Fat Bottomed Girls?"

Each of the pig's suggested titles were classified by his fellow runts as "Shit!"

"Did you find Sami accommodating?"

"Who?" the son asked, scrutinising his eye bags in the mirror.

The old man nodded in the direction of the girl behind the bar – she was currently pulling two pumps at once.

"Did you not enquire after her name, as would a gentleman?"

The son shrugged.

"Sounds like you did…"

The father sipped.

"I only had to read her name tag."

"Oh yeah? Eyes just happened to be drawn down that way, huh?"

Try as he might, the father failed to suppress the unveiling of a devilish grin.

"Jeez, she's young enough to be your carer, Pops…"

A smash.

Some "dappy fucker!" had dropped his glass.

The girl bent over and cleaned it up.

The workers were enthralled…

The son's phone buzzed – another text.

Followed by another in immediate succession.

Although it pained him to do so, the son began tapping a response.

A single message. To the point.

A quick dousing of the flames…

He was halfway completed when another text interjected.

Same sender. Same story.

The son deleted his reply…

"Uptown Girl?"

"Shit!"

"Power of Love?"

"Shit!"

"The food?" the father enquired, forced into raising his voice.

"No sign, Pops. I didn't have time to—"

Malevolently fisting the jukebox with blackened trotters, the lead pig announced he'd found the perfect choice.

It began like an eruption.

As did the accompanying terrace chants:

"I aaaam the one and own-a-ly!

"Can't take that-a-way from me!"

The son couldn't help but feel that the worker's warbles were directed in his and his father's direction…

Ten

"Diz-zey, my head is spin-er-ring!
  "Like a whirl-a-pool it ne-ver ends-a!
"You're maaaking me DIZ-ZEY!"

Much to the delight of the father, the piggies were still at it…

As though a broken tooth, he spat a nugget of scratching into the empty bowl on the table – it pinged like a bullet and landed on the floor.

Walking past while zipping up his flies, one of the workers trod it into the carpet.

The old man shot him a draconian scowl.

Once his attention was safely preoccupied with the jukebox…

The next track suggested:

"Two Become One?"

"Fucking behave!" came a snort from the litter, mouth overflowing with ale. "Them girl's proper fucking gash!"

"You got anything fucking better in mind?"

A maelstrom of peanuts were hurled across the room.

"Fucking anything better than that shit, you fuck!"

The father chewed his tongue – sneered with jawbone grinding.

The son recognised this simmering all too well:

Pops was becoming irascible, as black and ill tempered as a bear – traits exemplified by hunger, as his coveted roast was still nowhere to be seen.

But most of all, those hollering louts in the corner were beginning to grate on the old man's already tender persuasion…

"Kids." the son did his best to moderate, himself nearing the limit of his patience. "Let them have their fun. They'll soon head back to digging up the roads."

"You can splash 'em as we drive past, if you like."

The father implied, given the chance, he'd do more than that…

"Just ignore them, Pops."

"They're not exactly making it easy!"

The uncivilised little piggies weren't. Mid-afternoon and their liquid lunch was still ongoing – round eight currently being gargled in the manner urinals are flushed.

How the girl behind the bar was managing to keep pace with their orders was a miracle – and considering the vile advances she was perpetually dodging, how she hadn't slapped one of them was equally as impressive…

As she collected their glasses, a worker made a reach for her thighs.

The father clenched his hands together as though cracking a nut.

"If I were twenty years younger…"

"Then they'd still drop you on your arse." the son felt safe in assuring…

If the workers weren't shouting their next orders at the girl, they were shouting their attitudes at each other – City and clunge the blue and the red of their own political spectrum.

And the volume of the jukebox had also been cranked high into the upper decibels…

"I suppose they've got to make themselves heard." the son winced, his own voice raised as a result. "Over the music."

"Music? Is that what that is?" the father grumbled sarcastically. "And there was I thinking a plane had crashed."

The son took a drink.

"We could always head back." he reasoned – although he didn't relish spending the remainder of the afternoon in that cramped hospital corridor, it would at least give the old man one less thing to complain about.

Besides, the son got the impression that his father was the focal point of the workmen's roaring laughter – the butt of their inside, puerile jokes.

"What do you say?" he encouraged. "Best we make a move?"

The father stood firm, chin pronounced.

"We've paid for our meals." he stated.

"They'd refund us."

That wasn't the point…

"There's food in the car." the son brokered. "And that cafeteria was qui—"

"We're not running away, David.

"We're staying."

"If that's the case," the son bucked, finishing his pint—

But his sentence was decapitated by a booming intro from the jukebox:

An intro known to all.

Known to the workers.

And known to the son, specifically…

A song from his youth. The soundtrack to his adolescence.

So loud and head-splitting it could summon the dead themselves…

"Fucking shit…" the son muttered spitefully, bringing down his glass. "I hate this song."

"That makes two of us." the father scowled in agreement.

He started to rise. Horns forward. Warpaint applied.

"Enough is enough. If no one's going to put a stop to this—"

The son asked that he leave it. Forget it.

"Let's ju—"

"It's you, ain't it?" came a gravelly insinuation.

Both father and son looked up.

A mound of fluorescent gut glared back…

Beer in hand, phone in the other, the heaviest of the workers had come to lord it over the men's table as though it were a grave he'd excavated.

"Yeah." he asserted, brimming with pride at his plundered discovery. "I knew I recognised you hiding over here – knew it the first time I saw yer."

He put his pint down on the table, pushing the son's to one side. From the corner of his mouth he called-out to his mates, never for a moment taking his eyes from the two men below him.

"Oi, John! Didn't I fucking say it was him!" he shouted over the clamour of the jukebox, a cloud of sputum bursting forth. "That bloke from years back!"

The son noticed his father shift awkwardly in his seat.

"John!" the worker barked again, that vile Northern accent which resembled vomiting. "John! Fucking John! This cunt here! Didn't I say it was him!"

The father was locked tight. Unflinching yet incapable of retaliating.

The son found himself speaking in his defence.

"You've got the wrong idea, mate. We're just two nobodies having a quiet drink.

"At least we were trying to…"

"Nobodies or not," the worker said, eyes fixed on the old man, "you used to be that guy, didn't 'cha."

"Don't think he was." the son argued.

"Yeah. From back in the day."

"Not him, mate."

The worker suddenly turned and dug a hard blistered finger into the son's chest – right between his ribs.

"Yeah. You're that David." he said, certain of his subjects identity. "That David Jr. fella.

"From that band."

The jukebox seemed to blare louder.

The son vented through his nose.

"And me and the lads just wanted to say," the worker grinned, all fried onions and stubble, chin inches from the son's nose. "This old record of yours, this old banger…

"We.

"Think.

"It's fucking.

"Shit."

The son clenched his fists – ears ringing, blood coursing.

He looked down at the finger embedded in his chest – one more poke and he was going to break it off.

And everything else in-between…

"Yeah, he's David." the father interjected suddenly.

The worker turned his head, still smiling that idiotic smile.

The father fixed him dead in the eyes:

Fuelled up.

Hackles erect.

Eyes as blue as a blowtorch's flame.

"He's David, alright…

"And who the fuck are you?"

That idiotic smile soon paled…

Judging by the swiftness in which the worker took his leave, both father and son agreed he was no one worthy of recognition.

Eleven

The long-awaited roasts were set upon feverishly. Heartily. Two sets of fighting irons all 'a blur and 'a clatter.

And the meal was sumptuous beyond comparison. Every bit as delicious as hoped for.

Especially now that the gastropub had been reunited with its original fireside tranquillity.

Now that the oinks had kindly fucked themselves off into the rain…

"You know," the son mumbled through a mouth compacted, "I can't remember the last time I heard you swear."

The old man tutted.

"Must have been years ago." the son continued, mashing a roasty with his fork.

"Decades, even. That Christmas I broke the punch bowl?

"Or the time with the cabbage whites and the greenhouse? Remember that?"

The father dissected a parsnip.

"You went ape-shit!" the son laughed. "Mouth like a fucking machine gun."

"One shouldn't make a habit of profanity, lad."

"You should.

"It suits you."

"I find it ill fitting – repugnant for one such as myself." the father replied haughtily.

"However, when means are a must," he grinned, a piece of rosemary caught between his teeth, "I can tear it off with the best of them!"

When the old man orated, his audience only heard a voice bred of heritage.

Born of the theatre – pruned and clipped with the exactness of a vicarage shrub.

Not like the son; a shabby fiddle to his father's violin. He accentuated his bottom rung Manchurian tones – proudly, forthrightly, nasally, a working class chip on his shoulder worn like a rosette.

But not the father. Pickled Peppers and Yellow Lorries and Father's Father's Jaguars – he could deliver them as immaculately as an artist sculpts bosoms from marble.

Yet rarely in the accent of his birth.

And never when his blood was up…

Only the son was able to decipher the old man's paraded elocution – the rare slips of the tongue his father had spent years trying to conceal were, to the son's ears, as stark and contrasting as duck confit ladled with Henderson's relish…

As he ate, he listened closely while the old man regaled with swashbuckling tales of his younger years, all belt buckles and sabres, midnight chandeliers, and skulls held aloft under limelight.

Those 'U's so frequently stepping upon the toes of his 'O's.

"…when Ms. Taylor sent the dishes flying c'u'me the end of the party, I chose wisely to d'oo'k…"

And after all these years, after all the dress rehearsals, the father still dragged and doubled his 'A's when a single 'I' would have sufficed.

"…I still believe, and will do until my dying day, that m'a'ght is never r'a'ght…."

As they say: You can take the boy out of Manchester…

"You did well to keep a lid on yourself earlier." the father remarked, wiping his mouth with a napkin. "In your younger years I imagine, and well recount, that the situation would have escalated all too rapidly."

The son shrugged. He crushed another potato.

"You've mellowed with age." the father maintained.

"I've aged alright…

"My fuse's still short.

"Just damper…"

"But you didn't lose control of yourself. You remained calm when antagonised.

"You showed restraint."

The father took to his water, holding it to his lips for longer than organic.

"That, my lad, is a quality to be admired…"

Melancholic, the old man stared off into the distance.

To the bar.

The mirror.

The paintings.

And then the jukebox – it was currently cycling at random, its volume sedated.

"I know that song meant a great deal to you, David." the words necessary yet difficult to form. "I know how much of yourself you poured into the writing of it."

The son scoffed disparagingly, consuming at a pace.

"Yeah, it made me a few quid, if that's what you meant."

The father placed his glass down.

"I didn't…"

"Do you remember how old you were when you wrote it?"

"Wouldn't know." the son evaded. "Can't remember that far back."

"Try thinking back." the father encouraged.

The son exhaled, disconnected eyes weighed down at his plate.

"Well, came out spring '92…" he chewed.

"Hit massive that summer…

"So that would make me, what, twenty at the time?

"All a bit of a daze, if I'm honest. White fog, you know…"

"You were fourteen." the father corrected with conviction. "I know you were fourteen because I still have the birthday card you wrote the original lyrics on."

This admission surprised the son – although he masked such a reaction with a display of indifference.

"That far back, huh…

"And you've had it all this time?"

The father nodded.

"Well…" the son remarked, posturing apathy. "Must be worth something."

"A great deal…" the father replied heavily…

"Yeah, I remember the card." the son eventually admitted, looking up from his plate. "A big drawing of a champagne bottle, with 'From a Pop to his Son.' in an airbrushed font."

Correct. The father recalled it that way, also.

"Covered in that cheap glitter that rubs off on your fingers." the son reminisced. "Like blue sand. Got right under your nails."

Blue sand. That was the lad!

"And blank…

"Empty…" the son stated thickly.

"Not a fucking word inside…"

And this single detail the father remembered more vividly than any other…

As though spontaneously materialised, the girl from the bar arrived at the men's table.

Beaming, she presented two immaculate pints.

"Here you are, my men." she announced, setting the drinks down. "Complements of the house."

Finding himself somewhat delicate at this moment, the father feigned distraction in his meal.

Equally, the son's first words were frangible and confined.

"And for what do we owe the pleasure?" he asked.

The girl grinned, puffing out her chest.

"For sending our noisy friends on their fucking way, that's what!

"We've been wanting to say that to them for weeks." she enthused, addressing the father. "And thanks to you, it's about time somebody did."

Countenance restored, the father almost blushed at such adulation. Almost…

"Well, it was nothing, my dear." he twinkled, setting down his cutlery. "I'm just glad my theatrical arsenal could be of service."

The son rolled his eyes.

The father told him to hold his knife properly.

Not like an ape…

"I would hate you to think I regurgitate language of that nature on a regular basis."

"Wouldn't mind if you did." the girl excused. "If it keeps customers like that away then all the better.

"We could use you in here most Fridays, if I'm honest."

"You'd have to speak to my agent about that!" the father laughed.

Although she chuckled politely, it was clear that the girl didn't get the joke.

Before her time…

"Anyway, I'll leave you both to your meal – and if you need anything else, anything at all," she said, drawing attention to her name badge, "Just ask for Sami."

"Sami." the father repeated, a close inspection to ensure that the name was indeed correct. "You're too kind. Thank you again, my dear."

"Ditto." the son added, wryly.

The girl smiled at him over her shoulder…

As she departed, the two men shared banterous glances – then slowly turned their attention towards the two monolithic elephants in the room…

The son was first to break the silence.

"Like I say," he said, taking one of the pints for himself, "You should swear more often."

The father nodded vaguely, his attention harnessed on the remaining pint.

With a shake of his head he withdrew himself.

He focused on his meal.

The surroundings.

But only in guise.

"I'm guessing it's another of the Lancs." the son reasoned, picking up a spud with his fingers.

He twisted it in gravy.

"Goes well with the beef – wasn't that what you said?"

The father chewed said beef.

"You take it if you want, lad."

"Only if you won't."

"It's yours, David."

"You earned it, Pops."

The father took to his water.

It was almost empty…

"Alright, I'll call time on it." the son chuckled, putting up his hands before reaching over towards the glass.

He'd had his fun at the old man's expense.

"I'll see about getting you another wate—"

"No!" the father expelled, his hand slapping his son's away.

With knuckles white he snatched at the pint, clenching it towards his chest.

For a moment, as though a chalice, he clasped it in both hands.

"No…" he repeated. "No, that won't be necessary."

"You're sure?" the son reasoned soberly, rubbing his hand. "I was just pissing with you."

As though blinkered, the old man didn't reply.

"What about the car? Driving back? Parking?"

The father registered these dilemmas briefly – but the hurdle had long since been leapt.

"It's just the one drink." he uttered, the arguments spoken into the glass.

"Big meal. Watered-down.

"It won't effect me.

"And after all that's happened today," he concluded, his most telling excuse, "You'll agree that I deserve it."

The son looked on as his father brought the pint to within the reach of his lips.

Elbow bent.

Glass tipping.

Eyes closed…

But then the father stopped – considering his son's mindful and apprehensive gaze over the rim, he ensured the pint went no further.

Yet it didn't hurry back to the table, either…

After what felt like a lifetime for both men, the father leant across the table and poured the contents of the glass into the plant pot beside his chair.

He shook the glass vehemently, strenuously, being certain to dispel every last drop – and then he set it aside, pushing it to the table's edge, beyond his reach.

He ensured the son had seen him do so…

A tough slab of beef was chewed as though a stick of gum – the scrape of mastication and metal against china.

From the other side of the room, the jukebox hummed.

Rain fell gently against the windows.

The son supped his pint.

He felt guilty for doing so…

"Blue sand…" he eventually managed, picking at his fingernails.

"If you hadn't forgotten…

"Then I wouldn't have remembered."

Twelve

A clearing of the throat.
    "So, remind me again…
  "How long's it been?
  "Since you last, you know…"
  "Had a drink?"
  The father remained silent yet foreboding. As passive as a cornered rhino.
  Yet, along with his cutlery, his resilience eventually came down at his plate.
  "Thirty-two years." he relinquished – a weary and disdainful expel.
  He wiped a thumb across his mouth, slowly chanting the numerals as though a eulogy.
  "Thirty, two, years…"
  He shook his head.
  The son did the same.
  "Must take some doing?"
  The father snarled, pupils rearing upwards.
  "You'd have no idea…"
  Without the courtesy of an explanation, the old man snatched up his glass of water, drained it, and stomped off towards the bar.
  The son drank as though taking medicine.
  "No…" he muttered.
  "I've no idea…"

***

The father was still at the bar – belligerent, wrought, shoulders hunched.
  Despite the jovial interactions from the girl, for once the old man was unspeaking…
  The son sat alone at the table.

Silently. In wait.

He manoeuvred with his fork the emulsified remains of his roast as though mixing acrylics.

He looked to the painting, its fiery yellow canvas.

"This takes me back..." he muttered, scenes of bygone years manifesting in the void between the bottles...

Formative years.

Lonely years.

Years in which, as a boy on his father's arm, he'd felt himself to be little more than a prop, an accessory, a talking point to necessitate the old man's interactions with the heyday glitterati – for fear that he'd have to quaff their bubbly on his lonesome...

Monday through Friday, the social calendar of the celebrity elite was relentless:

One night it would be a film premiere.

The next a wrap party.

Then a house warming.

An awards ceremony.

A preview.

By the time the weekend rolled around, any excuse for a piss-up was deemed merited...

And the boy had been dragged by the collar to all of them – school the next day or not. Such was the frequency of the soirées in those days, he had survived on little more than canopies for much of his childhood.

Although there was always plenty to drink...

As proud as the punch he was so fond of indulging, the father was forever eager to present his lad to his fellow thespians, exhibiting him as though a wind-up toy.

Look at this one! he'd call upon the guests, laughing hysterically while the child in the matching tux bore the brunt of everyone's sly politeness.

Come the party's end, however, and said offspring was soon forgotten...

Abandoned, he'd be left to find his own way home while daddy lay unconscious in a hedge, or behind the wheel – or splayed across the street in a puddle of his own piss, beneath the feral blaze of a dozen photographers' flashbulbs.

It was inevitable, like a moth to a flame, that the boy would be dazzled by their glare…

The son took a drink. A prolonged dosage.

The father returned with his own to hand.

"Lemonade." he stated gruffly, landing down in his seat.

"To cleanse the palette, if you must ask."

The son hadn't – he only saw a tall glass of clear liquid:

Fizzy. Iced. A shard of lemon.

Slightly cloudy…

Inflamed, the father offered it up, thrusting the glass under his son's nose.

"Try it if you don't believe me." he insinuated.

"I didn't say anything?"

"You were thinking it."

"Thinking what?"

The father considered any further response an insult…

In a huff, he returned to what remained of his meal.

The stuffing had solidified like rubber…

"So, come on then," the son pried, turning the old man's crank. "What's your secret? How do you manage to stay dry for thirty-odd years?"

The father refused to look up from his plate.

"Chatty all of a sudden, are we lad?"

The son cut a smirk.

"As we're blessed with this time together…"

Crabbish, the father took his time finishing his mouthful.

"I keep myself busy.

"That's all."

The son didn't believe that.

"Work?"

"That and other things.

"Your mother always has a chore ready and waiting."

The son ground his teeth.

"And what about when there aren't any chores?"

"Then I at least attempt to steer clear of temptations." the father said, motioning to the son's pint.

The son took a slug from it.

"Lunch was your idea, Pops…

"I'm guessing that's why we never went anywhere, after you went teetotal?" was his mordacious follow-up, asked with cautious yet deliberate provocation. "Never went out for dinner every evening like we used to?"

"That was partly the reason." the father admitted. "But I doubted any self-respecting teenager would have cared to spend their rare evenings on the town confined to the company of this old codger.

"I'd have cramped your style."

With this the son couldn't argue.

The brighter the spotlight, the greater the attention…

"And before, there was always a hubbub when we attended The Ivy" the father remembered.

"And The Ritz." the son in turn recalled. "For their Teas."

"That's right." the old man smiled, tittering to himself. "You could never understand why they cut the crusts off the butties."

"As would any kid." the son said, standing by this life-long stance. "Best part, the crust."

"And twenty-five pounds!" the father lamented. "Twenty-five pounds – in those days! And you only got half the bread."

The old man looked to his son, his face open.

"Such a waste…"

With this the son agreed…

"You know, the last time we had a drink together," he noted sombrely, comparing the two drinks on the table, "I had the lemonade, and you the beer."

"It's never too late to switch back." the father offered. "Or at least share the same.

"And this one will be on me."

The son considered his half empty pint – the dingy, cloudy contents.

And the radiant clarity of his father's fizz.

"If you're buying, Pops…"

Grinning, the old man was only too happy to race back to the bar.

Thirteen

"**O**pen wide, my lad!" the father thrust. "Here comes the choo-choo!"

"Batty old bastard!" the son bemoaned albeit playfully, flapping away the oncoming spoonful of rum and raisin ice-cream from the direction of his gob.

"People are looking, for Christ's sake."

But the father was undeterred by such vagaries – he was having far too much fun. Wicked and childish and irresponsible fun – cross-eyed raspberries and ticklish giggles befitting a toddler splashing in puddles.

Obviously a sugar rush induced by the second portion of ice-cream.

And the succession of innumerable fizzy beverages, least forgetting...

There were enough empty glasses on the table to rebuild the Crystal Palace...

Tender overflowing, the spoon returned.

"Now look at what you've done!" the son carped. "You've gone and gotten fudge all in my pop, Pops!"

In that case, the old man reasoned, it seemed only proper that he provide him a refill!

A fresh one! A top up!

And a quencher for himself, why not!

"I think I'll partake of the cream soda!" the father practically rejoiced, vaulting half-way across the carpet towards the bar. "Fancy giving it a go, my boy?"

"This one's sweet enough." the son replied, fishing with a spoon the raisins from his lemonade. "But, if you're still happy to pay."

"Can't take it with me!" was the gleeful reasoning...

"Fuck…

"I'll have two of whatever he's having…"

The old man had certainly rediscovered his spunk since this morning, the son considered.

And the merriment was doubtlessly genuine – spontaneous and from the heart rather than plagiarised from the head, the father joking and jesting without the blatant exertion of summoning the method.

In a moment of theatricality akin to dress-up, he'd even tried on his son's glasses.

He'd liked them. The tint. His spry appearance.

He may invest in a pair.

"I'll get you a chain to go with 'em." the son promised. "Something glitzy to off-set the tweed."

"That I'd like." the father said, admiring himself in the mirror. "Although your mother is rather fond of my current pair.

"Do you think she'd be accepting of a replacement?"

"I wouldn't…"

In turn, the son had sported his father's floral neckerchief.

Nah. He wasn't convinced…

"I look like a camp sailor. Like those bottles of bubble bath you used to get at Christmas."

"Matey!" the father laughed, pinkie supporting. "I always had a thing for the mermaid, myself."

The son hadn't been entertained by this side of his father for longer than he could remember.

The father of birthday cakes and sprinkles. Of vanilla and cherries.

The father of Christmas mornings and bank holiday swims – of deserted eventide playgrounds where nobody but the boy saw a grown man straddling a tyre swing, hooting and romping unabashedly for the sole merriment of his precious little lad.

But that father was a distant memory…

Lost to the years – last seen, one early weekday morning, being dragged across the rear seats of his agent's car.

As a teenager, the son had watched the departure from the front window:

No reciprocated wave.

No calls or letters permitted.

Ninety days. Without distraction.

Until the old man was dry…

In the meantime, the boy was shipped away to a Southern boarding school – for his own good, the relatives were keen to enforce.

For both your sakes…

It was only when the end of term finally came around that the son discovered an alternate, wizened incarnation of his father awaiting at the gates:

Top-buttoned. Clean shaven.

Fresh breath and not a hair out of place.

There was neither a hug nor an embrace to cement the reunion.

Only a cold, firm handshake…

"I barely recognised you." the son admitted to the old man standing at his shoulder. "You were so… laundered."

"I'll take that as a compliment."

As initially prospected, the term away had not straightened the son out.

Just the opposite, in fact…

But the father – he was so unimpaired and devoid of whimsy that one would've assumed he'd been the student remoulded in the art of manners…

"I promised myself," he recalled, "From that day forward I was to be a new man. A better man!

"No more gallivanting. No more mucking about."

He looked down between his shoes.

"No more booze…"

Inarguably, life was better following the separation, the son remembered – calmer, steadier, a desistance of the unpredictable and chaotic.

All at the expense of the swings…

"I turned a corner." the father added in the tone of achievement, rocking back on his heels. "From that day forth, I regained control of my life.

"I was free. Functioning. Propelled by an unsuppressed certainty.

"And most of all, above all else," he declared, "I was clean."

The son was sceptical of this last point.

"Clean, eh?"

"Clean." the father repeated, turning to look his son directly in the eyes.

"As a bloody whistle."

"Well hows about you give that a try now?" the son mocked, zipping up his flies. "Before you piss all the way to your socks."

"Fuck'in Nora! The bleach and now this!" the father cursed, stepping back sharply from the urinal. "Get me a paper towel, will you lad! Piss'll stain the suede!"

***

"So," the father enquired in an upbeat timbre – albeit with a flush of the reticent. "Let me ask you…

"How was school?"

The son couldn't help but laugh.

In reaction the father laughed also.

But not so broadly – a laugh more restrained, blotted with discomfiture.

And with good reason…

Across all the breakfasts and dinners and sarcastic welcome homes shouted up the stairs, it pained the old man to admit that he'd never considered to offer his son this one simple exchange.

Thirty-odd years after the fact may not have been the ideal time to pose such a question.

But, he reasoned, better late than never…

"How did you find it? The boarding school?" the father clarified once the son's laughter had diminished. "Down in Suffolk, wasn't it?"

"Sussex."

The old man shrugged, stretching his jaw.

"How did you find Sussex, then?"

"What can I say…" the son pondered.

"Strict." was his blunt summation.

"The beds were as cold as the meals. The tutors as wearing as their classes.

"And nothing, nothing," the son burped, "came before etiquette."

The father was at least grateful that he'd learned to half-cover his mouth…

"I'll say one thing for that old prison, though," the son amended, patting his chest. "They had an almighty music room.

"Massive, it was – big as a stadium." he recounted as though chronicling the wonders of a pharaoh's tomb. "And brimmed with every instrument you could ever wish for: Fenders, grands, shells, big-strings – the whole shabang."

"My deposit wasn't entirely wasted, then." the father added humorously. "One term would buy a semi these days."

"Don't bless your pennies, Pops. I didn't exactly excel in any of the other classes.

"Especially," the son admitted, "when it came to theatrics…

"As was expected of me…"

The father rubbed his nose.

"I never meant to enforce that on you, David.

"I just hoped, perhaps, should the subject have appealed, that you'd follow—"

"I know." the son replied earnestly. "I gave it a crack – it just wasn't for me.

"I've enough trouble pretending to be this tosser most of the time, let alone someone else…

"Ah, fuck it." he dismissed, sipping his drink. "Their loss…

"And anyway, even if I had the talent, I couldn't compete with the kids of nowadays."

"Nor could they compete with the stars of my generation." the father was proud to underline.

He undid a button on his collar.

"In my view, they simply don't have it in them.

"Gutless, some might say.

"Jelly babies – all cast from the same mould."

"There's a few decent ones, to be fair." the son contended:

"That fella from the war film.

"Big lad.

"Him with the teeth."

The father couldn't recall.

Following a quick Google search on his phone, the son displayed the actor in question.

As though summoning a horse, the father clicked his tongue.

"He was once my understudy."

"And the master's verdict?"

A sip from a proverbial goblet.

"He'll go far…

At the old man's behest, Youtube clips were recommended, shared, the son sidling up to his father's side as the footage of rosé and yore poured forth.

The father's eyes glazed over at the sight of:

"Dear, blessed Larry…

"Did I ever mention, when I was first starting out, how he and I would lunch together?"

"Once or twice…" the son sighed.

"He was holidaying with us when you first learned to ride your chopper." the father added.

Surprisingly, the son couldn't remember this.

"'Tis true. He convinced me to remove your stabilisers."

The son rubbed his elbow.

"That went well…"

"Just a scrape, you big girl's blouse." the father chuckled. "Besides, once you'd gotten into your stride we couldn't pry you away from that bike – up and down and around and around you went, long into the night.

"Larry kept the headlights of his Rolls on for you, so you could keep going.

"Ran the battery dead!" the father laughed. "Missed his flight back to Monaco as a result!

"Another drink?"

The son nodded, passing his glass.

"Monaco, eh?

"Sounds like I should've persevered with that acting lark all along…"

With the father heading back to the bar, the son did a little reminiscing of his own:

Days of amber. Nights of acid.

Masses swayed. Shouted down. Stages trodden like throats.

Waking up in the backs of vans on the A507 with pockets empty, fingers blistered, and ears still ringing from that third deafening encore.

Monaco it may not have been – but it was fucking bliss…

"Did you come to any of our gigs, back in the day?"

"This old man? In that motley crew?" the father jested, placing down two vanilla cokes. "I would've stuck out like a vicar's arsehole…

"Perhaps I should have snuck along, though – when you were initially making your waves.

"I have it on good authority that you were quite formidable."

"Were?"

Interjecting his umbrage, the son's phone vibrated – it caused the numerous empty glasses on the table to rattle as though under siege.

The son looked over:

It wasn't the hospital.

He turned the phone face down – yet it continued to ring, rotating clockwise and counter under its buzzing gyrations.

"Those spammers again?" the father enquired, dubiously.

"Who else?.." the son sniffed. "Their relentless. Sharks after blood.

"Wish they'd just take a hint and leave me in peace…"

"Then why not try telling them that?" the father suggested. "Tell them you're not interested. Put a stop to it."

"It'll only encourage them."

"Then hang up and sever yourself from them altogether."

The son seriously considered the father's advice.

He'd been contemplating such an action for some time…

But no.

Fuck'em.

"I wouldn't give 'em the satisfaction." he resolved, coldly…

Sparing the battery and the table's varnish, the call eventually disconnected.

The phone lay still. Motionless.

For now.

The son knew they'd call back…

***

Between their free-flowing conversations and libations, the girl from the bar arrived periodically at the men's table to collect their empties.

On each occasion, the old man awarded her a coquettish wink for her troubles.

And a chivalrous kiss of her hand – if she wasn't alert enough to withdraw it.

"Sly fox…" the son smirked conspicuously.

"Do you happen to have any children, Sami?" the father prodded, a pointed remark in the direction of his son. "If not, can I offer you one?"

The girl offered a scrunched and professional simper – as she left, the old fox stole a crafty perusal of her hutch…

Gently, the son set down his glass.

Cleared his throat.

A chary opening:

"So, how's she been?"

"Who's that?" the father asked vaguely, attention still occupied elsewhere.

The son glared – the point didn't need labouring.

"Oh, forgive me." the father twigged, ceasing his perusal.

"Your mother."

"Yeah, if you like…"

"How's she been coping?" the son pressed, grinding an ice cube between his teeth.

The father exhaled heavily, a slow comb of fingers through his winter hair.

A strand found itself plucked under the lip of his ring – the father untangled and twiddled with it.

"If I'm to be entirely honest with you, lad," he sighed, flicking the stray hair into the adjacent plant pot, "she hasn't been herself lately."

"How so?" the son delved. "Her mood? Manner?"

"It's not a presentiment I can adequately delineate." the father stated with an expression of the terminally mystified. "On the surface your mother would appear just the same as always."

The old man's eyes softened as though under-poached eggs.

"Like a porcelain doll." he smiled. "As raring and spontaneous as a bunny."

The son nodded – having spent time with her recently, he could confirm this perception.

"But these past weeks," the father darkened, rubbing his fingers together as though sifting for the answer, "she's been acting as mercurial as this bloody weather."

Without remark, the son could also confirm to this…

"I don't know what's with her, lad." the father pondered "She's not entirely herself – dimmer, some how?

"As though she's protecting something, and the effort is a drain on her spirit?"

Fist to mouth, the son suppressed the rise of a stripping cough.

"And I can't shake the impression," the father continued, "that, ever since we were given the news…"

He folded his arms. Sought his son's concurrence.

"You'd imagine she'd be happy, wouldn't you?

"Or at least relieved?"

"It effects different people in different ways, I guess." the son offered, pinching his bottom lip between his fingers.

"News like that, coming at this time." he furthered. "It must be a lot to process?

"I know I'd struggle with it…"

The father stroked his chin, drawing out the wrinkles in his neck.

It was a while before he next spoke.

"Perhaps you're right." he settled. "Maybe I square these situations from a different perspective?

"Maybe it's my age?"

The son scoffed.

"Can't help matters…"

The old man fixed him with a look.

That look…

"I don't anticipate departing this earth any time soon, if that was what you were implying?"

"You know it wasn't, Pops…

"But try and see it from her point of view. What's she supposed to do in a few years from now – however things turn out?"

"She's secure." the father enforced, straightening his back. "Comfort – I can promise her that. Whatever the future holds they'll be food on the table. Money in the bank. A house to come home—"

The old man's throat closed – his next words strangled away…

He shielded his gaze, turned it elsewhere.

His eyes moistened.

At times like these, the lad's glasses would have proved useful…

As best he could manage, the son offered words of comfort.

"It's those hospitals, Dad.

"This time of year – it always gets to you."

He swallowed.

"It gets to us both…

"You know," the son recalled, summoning his voice from the depths. "The first time I ever saw you on stage, you were doing panto."

The father listened, yet remained turned to the wall.

"Sleeping Beauty. Down at the old Hammersmith. I can't have been more than five at the time. To a kid in the front row that stage looked massive – like a great ship coming at you.

"I remember being so fucking terrified I almost crushed Mum's hand I was holding it so tight!" the son recounted, taut like a violin bow. "Especially when the lights came down – darkness, the crowd falling silent, this build of anticipation.

"I wanted so badly to get away. Run home. Be anywhere but there.

"But then there shone this spotlight—

"And out of the darkness, you appeared on stage—

"And started singing…

"Christ…" the son proclaimed, his words holy with awe. "I'd never heard anything like it.

"It was like… a magic, you know? So profound it knocked the fear clean out of me.

"For the entire performance I couldn't take my eyes off you – I followed you around that stage for every verse, every chorus, every lyric, just staring up at you."

The father's lip quivered.

"At that age I didn't understand acting or theatre or any of that." the son said, biting down on his lip so hard he could taste blood. "But it didn't matter, because, you know what I thought at that moment?"

The son took a breath.

"I thought: 'Whatever it is my dad's doing,

"'When I grow up,

"'That's what I want to do.'"

The father turned, removed his glasses.

"Tell me, David." he said, a voice weaker than a plea. "Honestly now. Spare me any lies.

"Was I a good father?"

The son felt himself perish.

"Sometimes…"

It was the most he could offer.

Yet it was all the old man could ever have wished to hear.

***

It was the son's round again.

He hadn't been keeping track or score or a running total or anything like that – but the tally felt about right.

Fifty-fifty either way.

Maybe sixty-forty?

Or perhaps seventy-thirty, in favour of the father?..

Whatever – the old man had been back and forth to the bar enough times for the both of them combined. Another round trip and, such was the progressive deterioration of the old bugger's gait, he might slip a hip.

Or succumb to diabetes, if the son's hypoglycemic migraine was anything to go by...

"Two pops for two boys." he requested in a loosened drawl, placing the empties on the bar, one per finger.

A chiming of glass from out back suggested that the girl was engaged in some menial task – but she promised to be with him when finished.

That was cool – no hurry. All was golden.

The son took a seat on one of the many vacant stools lining the bar, and waited...

The gastropub was all but empty now – everyone but the father and son, it would appear, had dilemmas to attend to. Just past six and the kids would need collecting, the paperwork filing, the dinner cooking, the unrelenting regimen of everyday life taking precedence.

The place would fill up again tonight, the son was certain.

Due to the unrelenting regimen of everyday life...

But for now, all was quiet.

Except for the feverish orchestration demanded of the jukebox...

The old man was currently pestering with it – running a finger up and down the titles while muttering to himself.

Decisions, decisions... what would the old man select? the son wondered.

Beatles over Stones – he'd stake his life on it.

Before they were fab, before the hair and hemp – before their disgusting intemperance, as the old man regularly deplored.

Cocking an ear, the son awaited the outcome of the father's selection...

Bells.

Bass line.

Bullseye!

Never in doubt...

"You two taking a voyage?"

The son looked up.

"All these lemonades you've been having." the girl quipped, having returned from outside – the son noticed she had a large bottle of scotch tucked under her arm.

"Doubling your doses of vitamin C, in case of scurvy?"

"Yeah, we've got a long voyage awaiting us." the son joked in return. "We set sail for the motherland later tonight.

"I won't lie to you, Sami – I don't know if we'll make it back."

"Well, in that case," the girl said, fixing the bottle of scotch into an empty optic, "It seems only right that I give you a departing gift."

Ensuring the bottle was secure, she took a shot glass and drew a sample.

"A tap of the admiral, so to speak." she winked, placing the half-full glass at the son's hand.

The son peered down at his reflection in the golden, amber liquid.

His fingers trembled…

"We're required to drain the pipe each time we replace the bottle," the girl encouraged, "so it seems a shame to waste it.

"It'll only get poured away, otherwise."

And to sweeten the deal, she promised that,

"No one will ever know."

Courtesy a formidable persuasive, the son picked up the glass.

Cupped it. Inhaled it.

The vapours teased at his nose.

He took a check over his shoulder – the old man was busy pirouetting.

"No one will ever know…" the son repeated to himself, the glass rising upwards like mercury in a thermometer.

He looked to his father again:

Merry. Jovial.

Genuine.

Clean…

"No one will ever know…

"Apart from me…"

And so, working against himself, the son set the glass back down, and politely declined.

"The admiral not to your taste?" the girl asked, a little put out.

The son shook his head, shoulders loose.

"No." he smiled contently, feeling himself alleviated.

"Those days are long behind us…"

While the girl poured the scotch into a sink below the bar, the son continued to watch his father dance:

Slow boogie. Jelly hips. Heel and toe two steps behind the beat.

A display of dad dancing at its finest.

The son was only thankful that no one was left to see it…

And the old man was audibly humming to himself – singing for an audience of one.

Never had a vocal been less cleanly delivered.

Yet never had one been delivered as cleanly…

"Top of the Pops…" the son giggled, warmed by such an affirming display.

"I'll tell you one thing, Sami." he quipped over his shoulder. "At least the fizz'll keep him fuelled up for another encore."

"That and everything else." the girl chuckled.

Distracted, the son didn't quite catch her remark.

"Say again?" he asked informally, turning back to the bar.

"Your dad over there." the girl nodded, reaching for two glasses. "He had a sly malt when he first came in.

"Same again, was it?"

The son was stunned.

Speechless.

Stupefied as though slapped across the mouth.

"Behave yourself." he challenged, a joking intention – yet the following questions tumbled forth like those of a child.

"You're sure?

"My dad?

"The one over there?

"He's had a drink?.."

This the girl confirmed without the gravitas her revelation had merited, nonchalantly slicing two wedges of lime.

In contrast, as though dicing onions, the son turned back to his father, pink eyes wide and unblinking…

Head cocked, mouth half open, the old man was keeping rhythm on the jukebox's side panels, thumping them like the buttons of a pinball machine.

Occasionally, swaying to the music, he'd topple back on his heels.

The regain of balance was delayed and laboured…

Come on, the son contended against his better reasoning – the old man couldn't be pissed:

It was all the sugar. The roast. The ice-cream.

Touch of a hypo.

Enough to effect anyone…

And wobbliness was a regular symptom of age.

Elderly weariness. That was it.

The girl was probably mistaken – a simple misunderstanding.

"Might have been two, actually?" she added from the distance.

"Or was it a double?"

A sudden and unexpected increase in tempo resulted in a mistimed jig.

"Two doubles?"

Old eyes in disagreement over their respective degrees of latitude.

"Three, even?..

"Double, triple, whatever." the girl rambled, dropping a slice of lime into each glass. "He polished the bottle off faster than I could replace it – and he's had plenty of the others besides."

Key change. Another stagger.

A foul and audible curse.

The son's heart skipped.

As did the next song…

Inconvenienced, the father halted his dancing.

He marched up to the jukebox. Eyed it down.

A shake of the cabinet didn't restart the track.

Neither did a kick.

And so, convinced that the perceived provocation justified his actions, the old man raised up his arm and struck the jukebox with the back of his hand…

The son flinched at the impact.

His shoulders knotted.

He felt breathless as though being suffocated…

The music beaten out of it, the jukebox restarted – and the old man merrily resumed his cutting of the rug, grinning with tongue in cheek.

Like a passenger departing on a cruise ship, he waved across the room to his son.

His hand was already starting to bruise…

Acting as though operated, the son found himself picking up the drinks and heading back to the table.

His legs had all but abandoned their rigidity.

"I'll put them on the tab, shall I?" the girl chuckled, wiping the knife clean.

The son didn't reply.

He left the glasses on the table.

Clasping his mouth, he grabbed his coat and phone, and hurried out into the rain.

Fourteen

A spark. A flicker. A flame.

A fizzle…

The son cupped his hands around the cigarette quivering between his teeth, intent on setting it ablaze – yet the wind and the rain outside the gastropub were simply too overpowering.

That and his hands were trembling – tremors induced not by the cold, but by disbelief.

Incredulity.

And anger…

A clenching and concussing and all-consuming anger which accompanied the son's discovery that he'd been lied to – that he'd been deceived by the devil's sympathy and his torrent of crocodile tears.

In a rage, the son hurled both the cigarette and lighter to the ground – as a consequence, a coughing fit nearly ripped his throat in two, dislodging the tracts of aspartame bile which clung to the roof of his mouth.

Gripping the gastropub's wall, he doubled up.

Out it all spewed:

The revelations.

The deceits.

The truth…

Why had he not recognised it earlier? the son lamented of himself – in hindsight, the old man's perfumed gaiety was so blatantly polluted that he may as well have been swigging directly from the bottle.

And spitting it back into his face…

Perhaps, the son contemplated, he hadn't wished to uncover the truth behind his father's revival? So desperate had been for a reunion with the father of years gone by, that maybe he'd subconsciously ignored the slurred messages of goodwill, the tipsy platitudes, as one pleads ignorance to the motives behind a spurious act of charity?

Instead, and not for the first time, the son had foolishly humoured the father's masquerade.

Joined with him.

Encouraged him.

Received him open-armed with drink in hand.

A big dumb smile for dearest daddy...

How gullible he now felt.

A gutless mother fucker...

Empty and exhausted, the son fell back against the outside window of the gastropub – it was made of distorted glass, mottled and imperfect as though a casting taken of an estuary. This made the glowing internals appear fluid, as though beneath water.

From the early-evening darkness, the son peered witheringly into the depths...

A contorted silhouette floundered beside the jukebox, bellowing mistimed lyrics from its pickled blowhole.

As though loading a harpoon, the son reached into his coat pocket and pulled out the bottle...

There followed a cough which made his eyes water – yet he hurried another mouthful, down past the label.

The silhouette only laughed mockingly in approval.

And continued its splashing...

Mid-swallow, the son's phone vibrated, demanding his attention.

With a wet thumb and without deliberation, he set the call to speakerphone...

"You won't take a hint, will yer?" he snarled, dotting the screen with amber spittle.

"I have to fucking shout! It's coming down!"

Like a ship in a hurricane, the son's head was already beginning to roll...

"...Elly, please." he practically whimpered, sinking halfway to his knees.

"I can't do this. Not tonight.

"Not after all that's happened..."

He filled his mouth.

"Because it takes the fucking life out of me, that's why!

"You do! The whole lot of you do! Cancer! Leeches!" he yelled as though into a microphone, lurching back and forth across his abandoned, waterlogged stage.

"Using me up!

"Burning me out!

"Tricking me!

"Deceiving me!

"Treating me like some kind of—

"What?

"Me?

"Drunk?

"'Course I fucking am! What else would you expect me to do?!"

The inevitable backlash – he garnered it little attention…

While the bitch barked and the bottle drained, the son squinted through the window:

Past the father.

To the bar.

The shapely outline of the girl standing behind it, her molten form lubricious within the glass.

The son took another drink, lips caressing the thread.

"Time's have changed." he scowled facetiously, eyes glued to the window. "I thought you used to find my darker side attractive?

"The passion? The rough?

"The blood and the booze pumping up inside you?" he taunted, rubber hips and jaw unhinged.

A peer through both bottle and glass.

The outline of syrup over thighs…

"You heard me!" the son slurred, leering down at the rain-speckled phone. "You're a big girl, you know the way out!

"Go running back to that kerb where I found you!

"Girls like you always land on their backs, anyways!"

Screaming from the receiver.

Spillage over chin.

The phone went down.

The bottle came up.

Mouthful.

Coughing.

Eyes to the window.

Blood to groin…

Along the wall, light was coming from a rear entrance leading back inside the gastropub.

Bottle in hand and rife with intention, the son began towards it…

Fifteen

Music was blaring – the jukebox cranked to maximum once again.

His glasses marled with rain, the son tripped against a crate of lager.

"This song…" he cursed, making his way through the gastropub's cluttered stockroom, leaving a trail of in-turned footprints in his wake.

"I hate this fucking song…"

Yet on this occasion, the son was alone in his opinion…

The father, it so happened, had grown rather accustomed to his lad's 90's chart topper – at this moment he was throwing some obscenely crazy shapes to it. Hips and knees, jive and scuff, aping the lyrics in that grotesque impression he found so amusing.

And, the son discovered upon reaching the bar, the old man wasn't dancing alone…

The girl had joined in with the fun…

Either ensnared or seduced, she swung from the father's hand like a fervent bridesmaid, tucking and twirling under the old man's zestful encouragement.

Her laughter indicated seduction…

That, and the father's neckerchief was stuffed between her cleavage…

Stalking pruriently behind the bar, the son emptied his bottle in a single gulp.

He refilled it from the nearest optic.

He'd take his pleasures when and how he would…

The father only noticed that the son had returned when the later slumped down in his chair, rocking the table out of place.

"For your listening and undying pleasure!" the old man announced, tipping the girl into a crude lady's stretch, aiming her at the son like a loaded cannon.

"May I introduce, in all his former glory!

"David!

"Atherton!

"Jr.!"

As though a rose, the father removed his neckerchief from the girl's chest with his teeth.

The son found her upside-down delectation, repellent...

When the performance had finally concluded, the girl made her way back to the bar.

"Wet out?" she panted, adjusting her top. "You're soaked to your boots."

The son let the droplets trickle where they may...

Off balance and out of sync, the father sniffed his neckerchief as though inhaling ointment.

Exuberantly, he grabbed his son from behind, arms spread around the chair like a scorpion's pincers.

The son stiffened. Turned to ice.

An overly spirited embrace was nonetheless endured.

"Where'd you run off to, you little scallywag?" the father asked, his breath spiked with chemical lemon.

The son answered plainly:

"Stuffy. Needed the air."

The old man laughed as though this were the funniest punchline he'd ever heard – a hissing and whistling from a rusted kettle.

Vice-like, the hug continued – white-knuckled across the son's shoulders.

The old man's ring dug into his collarbone.

"That's my lad!

"My fat little pygmy!"

The platitudes sloshed into his ear like poison...

The son eventually managed to wriggle free.

He pulled down his jacket, removing the creases.

He assumed his father hadn't felt the bottle in his inside pocket.

And even if he had, he couldn't give a fuck all the same...

The father returned to his side of the table. Unsteady as though at sea, he palmed his chair for balance, disguising the motion as a checking for dust.

"Ready for another?" he proposed, misshapen words from a numb mouth.

The son declined. His gaze remained lowered, his response barely audible.

"Ain't it about time we were getting back?"

The father didn't bother checking his watch. No need.

"The night is still young – plenty of time to get a few more down us."

"And what about dearest mother?.." the son sneered, breathing heavily.

The father laughed, making a point of rattling the cubes in his glass.

"They'll keep her on ice."

Such was the genius of his quip, the old man was initially blind to his son's disgust.

"Ahh, cheer up you miserable little sausage!" he cackled, bruised hand on hip, coming across all plastered Peter Pan.

"Make a night of it! Have another couple of drinks with old Pops!"

The son sniffed.

"Just one more, lad."

"No."

"Come on! Sami's offering her juices in every flavour of the rainbow. Peaches and passions and cherries and—"

"I said no, for fuck's sake!"

The father huffed.

Another of the boy's temper tantrums…

"Happy as Larry one minute, glum as midnight the next." he asserted with a look of accusing bemusement.

He waggled a demeaning finger in the vague direction of his son.

"I've never been able to figure you out, lad – you're too complex for me.

"A puzzle short a piece.

"A crossword missing a clue.

"A knot I'll never fully unravel…"

He smiled into his glass, preparing to drain it.

"Just like your dear old mothe—"

"She's not my mother!"

Silence.

The father was startled – frozen as though spat upon.

He soon thawed…

Ominously, he descended towards his son.

Lion wide. Rottweiler chest.

Forehead lowered and aimed...

He put down his glass – in doing so he misplaced it on the edge of a coaster. It fell on its side and rolled in a circle, spilling its contents.

Neither man noticed...

"What did you say?" the old man asked in a low, demanding tone, palms flat on the table.

The son bit his nails.

"You heard me, Pops."

"No, David, I don't think I did."

The son looked away.

"It doesn't need repeating."

"Oh, I think it does..." the father slurred, that accent returning to the cobbles of its creation. "Come now, be a brave little pygmy.

"Tell your father the truth.

"Before he loses his temper..."

Feeling himself beginning to shake, the son squared up.

"I said, you wasted old pisshead...

"That one in the hospital,

"This year's model,

"The one you care oh-so deeply about, that you'd never let anything happen to..."

He looked the old man square in the face, an inflexible voice unwavering yet fragile.

"She's not,

"My fucking,

"Mother."

Fire raging. Blood and oil ready to spill. An apocalyptic inferno rising within the father so great it could only manifest in the form of violence.

The son recognised this.

Had once feared this.

Yet he was unperturbed – desensitised.

No matter how enraged the old man became, the son knew he wasn't a child any more.

Now it would be a fair fight...

"You'll take those words back, my lad."

"Which part?.." the son smirked callously, practically laughing.

The old man turned a shade of scarlet…

"You'll show your mother the respect she deserves!"

"A mother who's less than half my age?

"She's barely a woman!"

"No less a woman than that pubescent little slut your shacked up with!"

The son exploded.

"At least I don't refer to her as your fucking daughter!"

The father soon followed…

"I wouldn't want a fucking daughter like that!" he roared, slamming his fists on the table. "I'd never tolerate a louse like her in the family!

"My family!

"A feral fucking tramp that wouldn't—"

Picking its moment, the son's phone buzzed.

"Perhaps that's her now?" the father suggested with a crooked sneer. "She senses her precious sugar daddy is in peril and has come running to his aid!"

The son practically tore the phone from his jacket pocket – still staring at his father, he swiped the screen and slammed it to his ear.

"And what does she have to say for herself?" the father berated. "Does she need money? Is that it?

"Do you need more money, Elly?!" he shouted across the table. "For rent? Heels? Extensions? A clean pair of knickers for the summer prom?"

The son put his hand over his ear, pressing the phone closer.

"No? Then maybe somewhere to rest your empty little head?

"We've lots of space back home!

"Settees! Recliners!

"Empty beds aplenty!

"And there's always room on the back seat of the car! You can curl up there if you like, and sniff where your fancy-man's arseholes have been!"

The girl came over and asked that they keep it down.

The son blanked his father's furious rebuttal – instead he listened intently to the phone.

With a growing distress.

A whitening face…

When the call had finished, he interrupted his father.
"That was the hospital." he said nervously.
"There's been 'complications'…"

Sixteen

D addy was home, back from the dead – the old man clambering up the stairs.

Only this time the son found himself without a bed to climb into.

Only a rapidly emptying bottle…

***

It had been going for ten minutes straight:

A crash of furniture.

An abandoning of decorum.

A ferocious tirade fired point-blank into the faces of the cowering nurses.

"Calm down?! You're expecting me to calm down?!

"You keep her from me!

"You lock me out like some criminal!

"And you honestly expect me to calm down?!"

Brutal. Demonic. A peeling away of the father's facade – that previously pruned and botanical accent now culled of its gentility, the old man's roars reverberating down the hospital corridor like a dozen pickaxes swung angrily into coal.

This was no longer a gentleman – a man of repute.

This was a creature at its most animalistic – a powerhouse of insinuations and intolerance and turmoil which no one surviving the hospital had the bravery to contest.

Least of all the son…

As always, when finding himself mired in these situations, he'd chosen to flee – hunkering inside the corridor toilet, back against the door, a little boy under the covers with teddy and torch.

Clasping tightly to his bottle…

Yet no matter how copious, alcohol was an ineffective pacifier – the son knew that the father's eruption wasn't going to diminish anytime soon, for experience had taught him that a fire rages until nothing remains for it to consume.

And he had the scars to prove it…

"By all means – you call those up on high!" the beast outside roared, all talons and flame.

"If they've got a problem, then bring them!

"Let them face me!

"Then we'll all have a r'a'ght fucking tear up!"

The son assaulted another swig, taking the bottle to its bottom third for the second time this hour.

Light headed, queasy, he leant his hands on the sink.

He peeled away and tossed his glasses to the side – bowed his throbbing forehead against the mirror.

He felt he might throw up. Pass out.

He may well do both…

Self medicating, the son charged the taps and slapped a handful of cold water across his face, rubbing it vigorously.

When that failed, he took another long, vertical swig.

Another long, excruciating cough.

Another contemptuous stare at his pathetic reflection in the mirror.

The reflection stared back – marble, judgemental eyes.

The bombardment grew louder.

"All this is your doing!" it came, emboldened and stretching further North by the octane. "You know that, don't you!

"Of course you know! You're not stupid! You understand all that you've done to my wife!

"You know that if she dies in there, on that slab with her legs apart, then the blame will lay solely on your shoulders!"

The face dropped. Sneered.

The son half expected it to turn and abandon him to his fate.

"And I'll make sure you never fucking forget that!"

The old man had been right all along, the son considered:

Swearing didn't suit him…

***

The father had driven them back to the hospital in a blaze of exhaust and cylinders – a blind man shovelling the furnace of a runaway train.

Corners were cut. Lights run. Abstract trivialities such as lanes and limits considered irrelevant by his heavy right foot.

For the old man was driving under duress.

Fury.

Terror.

The terror that he wouldn't make it.

The terror that he'd be a few seconds late.

And the terror, should grace permit that he arrived in time, of not knowing what horrors would inevitably await him…

When the father and son finally arrived at the hospital, the nurses weren't of much help. They could only try to explain the situation. Keep the son informed.

And the father subdued.

Their pandering only made things worse…

Mugs were thrown. The plastic bench upended.

Hands at their belts, two security men had been called to intervene.

The nurse behind the desk had also pleaded with the old man, trying to appeal to his punctilious side.

Perhaps he'd like to sit down? Cup of tea?

Go somewhere quieter?

Would he fuck!

Had he been in his younger years he'd have brought this whole fucking place down around them!

And now, a further ten minutes later, the foundations of the hospital were still being threatened…

***

A flush.

A cough.

A rinse of claret from the mouth.

Gingerly, the son eased open the toilet door.

Grasping it for stability, he squinted to the opposite end of the corridor from which the father dominated.

The doors to the ground floor beckoned.

Leading down.

Outside.

Away.

The son turned back to his father – fire and thrashing and fingers of culpability.

Then the doors – freedom, escape.

Abandonment…

He couldn't bring himself to face the former.

Nonetheless, the time had passed to make a dash for the later…

On the warpath, weaving between the walls, the father came storming down the corridor, still shouting vile and unfounded accusations at the staff.

One of the buttons on his shirt had come undone at the belly, while the shirt itself was halfway untucked.

Sweat trickled from his top lip.

His neckerchief was nowhere to be seen…

He snapped around to face his son, almost knocking into him.

Both men did well to maintain their balance…

"Where the hell have you been hiding?" the old man demanded, teeth bared, breath flammable.

"Piss." the son slurred, letting the toilet door fall closed with a bang.

"Great! That's just marvellous!" the father wailed sarcastically. "Fat lot of good you are!"

Despite his next words being intended for his son, the old man swung back to the staff.

"They won't let me see her!" he said, mortified at the very idea.

"Me!

"Her lover!

"Her husband!

"This boy's fucking mother!" he yelled, hand cupped to mouth.

The son barely maintained his composure…

The two security guards were eyeing he and his father with a palpable sense of umbrage – and the son, through the mist of his drunken haze, was fast becoming aware of inquisitive faces sprouting from beds and peering around doorways, captivated by the unfolding drama…

It wasn't long before the son recognised that familiar burning of whispers in his ears – the scornful tuts and disapproving head shakes which the father's antics had a tendency to attract. There arose within him that overwhelming sensation of being judged as an accomplice – of being stranded on an empty stage and unable to speak.

The father's spotlight blazing directly into his eyes...

"Come on, let's get some air, huh?" the son urged, putting a hand on his father's shoulder. "Give the doctors space to do what they need to."

But the father slapped the hand away as though an insect.

"Off me, lad! I don't need taking outside!

"Not by you!

"Not by anyone!" he yelled again at the staff.

"Then at least keep your voice down, will yer!" the son hissed. "Before you get us both into trouble."

"Is that what concerns you, David?" the father inculpated with a mordant derision, a mocking brine to each of his words. "Trouble?

"Are you troubled by trouble?

"Confrontation no longer to your taste?"

The son threw up his hands and began staggering away.

So be it. Leave the old fucker to his fate. He had nothing left to say to him.

Oh, but the father had plenty...

"You always were a cowardly little shite!" he blasted after his son, practically stepping on the backs of his heels. "No fight in you! No enterprise!

"Jelly boy! Milky bar bitch! When the going got tough you'd always run home with tail between your legs, begging your famous pappy to make the world go away."

People were stopping their conversations now. Gathering in doorways.

Blocking any escape...

"Perhaps that's why you made up for your juvenile timidity in your adolescence?" the father accused. "Oh yes, all big and brave when you grew a bit of meat on your shoulders, weren't 'cha. Two fistfuls of excess weight which you were more than ready to swing at anyone who remotely critiqued you."

More ears. More eyes.

The son could feel the heat blushing in his cheeks.

"If you were too high to remember the headlines your malfeasance attracted then I certainly wasn't!" the father went on, the corridor his floor, the gathering crowd his turnout. "No, not I! Not the famous father! I remember them all too clearly!

"'Thug!' the front pages read!

"'Lout!'

"'Disgrace!'

"Pupils dilated! Blood down your face! Hands cuffed at your back!" he mimicked, wrists together. "Being hauled away like vermin!

"Yes, that's him!" the father mocked with Shakespearian bravado, eyes to the forth wall. "There he is! That's the lad! That's the spawn of these fair loins!"

Shaking with rage, the son continued walking away – his father's insults only dragged him back…

"A convict, ladies and gentleman!

"Top of the Flops!

"A one hit wonder imprisoned in a one bed cell before the first royalty cheque had even been smashed!

"…I mean – cashed!"

Disenabled by his drunkenness, the father attempted to correct himself.

"Before that first…

"Before their first…

"…before the first cheque had even been—"

Incensed by his inarticulate cloddishness, the old man took hold of a nearby painting and sent it ricocheting down the corridor.

The exertion carried him into the wall, leaning and wheezing like a punch-drunk boxer against the ropes.

The son turned around – considered helping his father up.

Or putting him down for the count…

Sensing the boy's diffidence, the father laughed to himself.

He spat on the floor.

"Take in the mutation before you." he invited of all in attendance, heaving himself from the wall, swaying between stewed ankles.

"Remember it. Learn from it.

"Learn from a father's mistakes.

"The result of only one pair of hands on the rod!"

"Don't make me…" the son warned.

"I never made you do anything!" the father tore back in his face. "And look what happened!

"Fat and wasted! Bloated and pathetic! Clinging with your fingernails to a bygone decade you neither effected nor featured because of your own childish susceptibility!

"I'll tell you, lad – there's so much in you I despise in myself!"

A grinding of tonsils. A tunnelling of vision.

The old man lurched over. Snorted. Sniffed.

"Yes, there on your tongue!

"Don't try lying to me, lad." he accused. "I can smell it on your breath like shit on carpet!

"You reeking little drunkard! You've been drinking again, haven't you?"

"Yeah! I've had a fucking drink!" the son exploded before all and sundry. "I'll admit it…

"If you do the same!"

Rather than contest this evident assertion, the old man only shook his head to the crowd.

"He knows full well I gave that up a long time ago." he belittled, the concept laughable.

"I gave up on all of it…

"The fame.

"The cheers.

"The adulation and applause I roundly deserved."

The father pointed an unsteady finger at his son.

"And all because of you…

"You!" he repeated, an accusation, a judgement of culpability.

"Because who else was left to look after you?.."

Reaching his crescendo, steeped in perspiration, the old man came to within an inch of his son's face.

He looked him in the eyes, and muttered his final death-dealing pronouncement:

"I'm only thankful your mother didn't live to see what you've become…"

That was it – the line had been crossed.

In a single bound, the son grabbed his father by the collar and rammed him against the corridor wall.

His hands were soon around the old man's throat, tightening of their own accord. Teeth clenched and berserk with rage, the father dug his fingernails into his son's wrists, attempting to detach their grip.

But, overpowered, he couldn't respond.

He was no longer strong enough.

The boy had outgrown him…

And so the old man found himself lashing out – a wild and reactionary fist neither aimed nor premeditated.

Only fuelled.

It struck the son across the nose.

The father felt the cartilage compress under his knuckles…

The son immediately recoiled, hands clasped over his face.

His eyes began to water…

The father froze, beholding the spectre of an innocent child.

Wet eyes.

Blood soaking into pyjamas.

A broken nose that would forever act as an indictment…

Panicked, the old man pushed the spectre away, two hands driven forcefully into the boy's chest.

The son flew backwards against the opposite wall, the back of his skull knocking a painting to the floor.

The frame smashed. Glass everywhere.

Attempting to break his fall, the son inevitably spliced his hands on the broken glass, leaving bloodied fingerprints streaked across the polished surfaces.

He felt a sharp penetration at his chest.

The father felt sick.

The two security guards had seen enough…

One grabbed the son under the arm, hoisting him to his feet.

In agony the son lashed out, a flailed elbow causing blood to speckle the walls.

"Get the fuck away from me!" he demanded, his voice constrained by the bleeding of his nose.

The guard refused, only gripping the son tighter – yet with a yank he broke free, stumbling halfway between kneeling and standing as he attempted to run.

The guard went in for a tackle.

"Don't you dare touch him!" threatened the obscured frame of the father, himself pinned against the wall by the second guard. "You lay a finger on my son and I swear I'll—"

But it was hopeless.

There was no putting the cork back in the bottle.
The son had long since abandoned him.

Seventeen

Swept and rudderless under a momentum he had no ability to dissuade, it was inevitable the son would slip the moment his trainers impacted the mulch surrounding the hospital car park.

He finished stooped on his knees – lacerated fingers submerged in feculent puddles, hyperventilating irregular plumes of condensation into the night.

Here he remained.

Shot. Spent.

Incapable of standing.

Cold rain pelted his back – like wax it trickled across his field of vision, dripping to the ground in thin gluey strands.

Carried with the rain, seeds of blood fell from his broken nose – the roots bled outwards from his sleeves.

Had the hospital car park not been bathed in a sodium orange light, which made everything indistinguishable in tone, the son would have been aware of a red mass expanding around him, his blood tainting the shimmering water.

But he could not have cared less – he was out of it, the surrounding world illusory.

In every puddle he only beheld the reflection of his father – the sound of each raindrop translated as a barrage of the old man's criticisms and condemnations of all his countless embarrassments.

And how the son had never, not once, engaged his father in retaliation against them...

Not until today. Tonight.

And how had he done so? he chastised of himself. How had he sought to rectify a lifetime of grievances?

With violence.

Drunken, unflinching violence.

Like father,

Like fucking son…

Crestfallen and bedraggled, the son struggled to his feet.

With a grunt he cracked his nose back into place – it was as numb as dead flesh.

He lifted his face to the sky and swayed drunkenly under the pouring rain, his t-shirt and clothing mantled.

Water streaked from his face, over his cheeks.

He may have been crying…

Unremitting, even at this moment, his phone rang.

To presume the caller would not require the son to check.

And to answer would only serve to condemn him further…

Thus, in an act of primal abandon, the son drew back his arm and without looking hurled that bastard phone into the ether…

The glowing obelisk spiralled wildly against the heavenly pitch like a falling meteor.

Far out, it landed with a crash. A shatter.

A harsh and wide-reaching light began flashing from the far end of the car park, creating stark and intermittent shadows against the surrounding bonnets, buildings and trees.

A car alarm…

In any other instance the son would have fled as though his freedom depended on it – but in his present inebriation he was nonplussed, deprived of awareness as though anesthetized.

If anything, he was curious as to who's car he'd hit.

Hobbling deeper into the pulsing light, he soon discovered whom the vehicle belonged to.

Who else?..

Tawny gold.

Lavished with leather.

And a split in the windscreen the length of a stratocaster.

A thing of fucking beauty…

Flinching at having cut his finger on something sharp, the son retrieved the bottle from his inside pocket:

The rim was cracked, snapped at the neck, replaced with a crown of daggers.

When he shook it, fragments of glass rattled inside.

Ignorant to the risk, the son took a celebratory drink from the splintered bottle all the same, toasting the scene before him as an arsonist would a blazing churchyard.

And by some farcical good fortune, the son discovered that his phone was still alive, also...

There it laid, on the concrete, beside the front tyre, struggling to be heard over the car's alarm.

Yet still it cried out.

Ceaselessly. Incessantly.

The glower of that lecherous bitch peering up at him...

A single stamp to her face quietened her.

A second, darkened.

And the third killed the phone altogether, the screen cracking under the son's heel, the battery bursting from the shell like the entrails of a cockroach.

Following a slug for a job well done, the son aimed his attention towards the car.

Pops' pride and joy.

His beloved treasure.

His precious little baby...

Standing directly in the glare of its flashing headlights, the son raised up his leg...

And brought it down upon the car's bumper with a mountain's worth of fury.

Again.

And again.

One for the road.

Two for the return.

And a third for good measure!

The onslaught soon snowballed...

There came ferocious kicks to the doors. Knees driven into the door panels. Boots lashed against hubcaps. Then knuckles, fists, punches, elbows, each attack leaving a residue of the son's blood on the paintwork as though the very flesh of the car itself were being lacerated away.

When the son's body surrendered it serration, the blunt base of the bottle took care of the windows, the wing mirrors, the chrome, the lights – each unceremoniously buckled and destroyed.

In all the chaos the son was unconscious to the fact that he was laughing at the top of his lungs – nor was he aware that he was swearing, screaming, cursing his father's name for all the journeys they'd taken together in this hellish little shitbox.

Never talking. Never sharing. Always arguing.

Strangers coming and going and leaving and returning to a half-empty house which neither considered home – the lights dimmed, the heating off, the doors closed.

The father collapsing onto his side of an empty bed.

The son cocooning on the bottom bunk while the top remained forsaken.

Both awaking each morning with red eyes and damp pillows.

Alone and abandoned to a life with each other…

Knuckles of bone stripped of their flesh, the son prepared one final assault on the car.

With an impact practically seismic, he brought the death blow down upon the bonnet.

The headlights burst.

The suspension collapsed.

And but for an internal, mechanical death rattle, the car's alarm fell silent…

Burnt out and clutching for breath, the son laid across the bonnet.

He took another drink from the bottle.

He cut his lip on the rim.

He hardly noticed…

***

When the son awoke after a period impossible to judge, he slid himself from the car's bonnet under a lubricant of blood, sweat and rain.

Getting to his feet, he found he could barely stand.

Yet he was braced by the pride resulting from his masterpiece – the disfigurement he had inflicted to his father's most treasured possession a nourishing sustenance.

Yet it did not sustain him long.

Such dismantlement had drawn up a thirst which only the bottle could quench…

A toast! the son announced.

To life!

Death!

And to all who entertain her!

The son hoisted the sharp end of the bottle to the stars, cocked back his throat, and prepared to drink his fill…

But a figure intruded upon his ritual – an uninvited guest postponing the climax.

"It's you again, ain't it?" croaked a voice as wretched as hot gravel.

The son turned, eyes delayed, bottle still to lips.

"Yeah, it's you alright." grinned a set of gnashers from the darkness, shining bright like chevrons. "I'd fuck'in know it was you anywhere."

There stood before the son a pair of bare arms ignorant of the cold. Belly foremost.

A backpack in one arm and hard-hat tucked under the other.

Unmistakably, it was the largest of the workmen from the bar.

And he had intentions of concluding his earlier altercation…

"Fancy finding you out here." he approached, a skid mark of a snarl across his face. "In this here car park. In this here weather."

He dropped his hat and bag together on the concrete, his boots treading a path of wet cement.

"Yet here we are. Just you and me, out here all on our lonesome…"

The worker stopped a few inches from the son, hands gripping his belt.

He smelt of hot tar – cheap deodorant and cheaper lager.

Amusingly, half a county's worth of cement dust seemed to have accumulated on his face.

Yet, the casting night made him appear wider than before…

"Bit of a mess you've gone and made for yourself." he assessed, peering over the son's shoulder at the wreckage once a car. "Right sorry state, the both of yer.

"Owner ain't gonna be happy about this."

"They'll get over it." the son responded.

"Guess you don't want the police involved?" the worker laboured, making a point of massaging his knuckles.

"No inquiry.

"No inquest.

"No fuss that can't be—"

"What d'you fucking want?" the son slurred.

The worker both intimidated and bored him. A domesticated silverback – dopey, blundering.

Yet unmistakably lethal…

Under the cracking of sockets, the worker rolled his shoulders – stretched his neck from side to side.

Ominously, he widened his stance.

"That's good to hear." he grinned, the dust on his face refusing to wash despite the rain. "Wouldn't want any trouble from the authorities now, would we?"

The son shrugged, shoulders lopsided and unsynchronised.

He dropped his hands to his sides.

The worker raised his in eagerness.

As a dejected sailor rides headlong into the eye of a hurricane, the son only welcomed what trouble awaited over the horizon.

Trouble soon arrived…

A fist – tight, directed and unstoppable, flying towards him from the darkness.

This the son managed to narrowly avoid, in the same motion swinging out blindly with a dismissive arm.

There resonated a sound akin to the chiming of a bell.

Hollow on hard. Sharp against soft.

The son couldn't place it.

Seizing to a halt, the worker appeared bemused, also…

He trudged backwards and away from his opponent, a hand pressed to his head.

Regardless, the son egged him on all the more – taunting him, antagonising him, offering up his chin.

"Come on! Let's have it!" he demanded, dropping his hands once again, his body still primed for the not forthcoming fight.

Yet the worker only stepped away further, tame and disorientated.

In the desaturated light, the son was perturbed to notice a sudden froth emerge from the worker's left temple…

Constant it dripped. Downward. Plumb line. Between fingers.

Distress clouded the worker's eyes – dumb, blank eyes, gazing upwards as though looking out from the pit of a well.

Feeling himself begin to tremble, the son peered down at the bottle still clasped in his hand:

The bottom corner was chipped.

And had fresh, dust-infused blood on it…

For an age the son could only stare at the figure rocking under the rain – inhuman, petrifying noises began spewing from the hole once its mouth. Parts of words. Haunted mumblings as though possessed.

Under in-turned knees the worker's balance would bend then regain – like a radio transmission he would fade in and out of clarity, expressions of distress and uncertainty garbled together.

"I didn't… I was… I only meant to…" the son attempted to confess, but it was clear that the worker was incapable of hearing him – he was looking around the car park as though suddenly finding himself there, still clutching his bleeding head.

Then, as gradual as decomposition, he began walking away…

The son watched him go. Every horrid step.

The body ambling slowly. Robotically. Stilt-like legs ferrying the corpse towards the nearby trees.

Over the grass. Into the undergrowth.

Beneath the leaves and branches, the snaps of twigs.

Then silence.

Deathly quiet.

Nothing beyond the percussion of falling rain and the distant passing of cars.

Yet all the son could hear was the pounding of his heart, thumping all the way to his ears…

He looked around, head snapping left to right, a rodent paranoid.

No sirens. No silhouettes. No one watching from the seats of cars.

He glanced to the hospital's chequerboard of bedside windows – despite most being curtained or vacant, it did little to stave off his concerns.

Stupefied with panic, the son grabbed the worker's belongings and threw them into the nearby bushes – with his trainers he smeared the prints of cement left by the worker's boots.

In desperation he got down on his hands and knees and attempted to clean the concrete with his coat, praying the rain would help him. Save him. Rinse the crime and his sins away before the daybreak's judgement arrived.

In doing so, he caught sight of his hands:

Blood.

They were covered in it.

Dripping with it.

And resting within them, cradled like an abortion—

The bottle.

Stained and broken.

Cracked and fleshed.

The remaining alcohol watered down and tainted with blood.

But still it remained.

Just a mouthful.

Just enough…

The son sat down, resting against his father's car.

He closed his eyes.

Slowly, he brought the broken bottle to his lips.

Then slid it down to his throat…

"David."

The son looked up.

Standing under the rain, bathed in orange light, was his father…

The son immediately got to his feet – he didn't know why.

He tried to explain, to excuse, to confess – yet he remained mute.

With his eyes welling with tears, his legs buckled and he fell back against the car once more, coming to a rest on the crumpled bonnet.

Here he remained, head bowed, awaiting the worst punishment of all – the retribution of his father.

Yet, without a word, the old man calmly took a seat beside his son.

Leaning in, opening himself, he cupped an arm around him.

Close to tears, the son leant his head towards his father, anticipating the sanctuary of his embrace.

But it never came.

Instead, the father reached across and took the bottle from his son's hands.

He held it up to the light, examining the bloodied contents.

Then he drank.

All of it.

Every last drop.

When he'd finished he wiped his lips on his wrist, and tossed the bottle over his shoulder.

It shattered across the car park, twinkling embers mirroring the stars above.

"A boy." the father stated, looking to the constellations.

"Born of Cancer."

"And her?" the son could only offer.

The father didn't answer…
The rain continued to fall.
Nothing further was said.

~